JACK HIGGINS

Sad Wind From the Sea

HARPER

Harper
An imprint of HarperCollins*Publishers*
77–85 Fulham Palace Road,
Hammersmith, London W6 8JB

www.harpercollins.co.uk

This paperback edition 2009
2

First published in Great Britain by John Long 1959
Arrow Edition 1981
Reprinted 1982

A catalogue record for this book is
available from the British Library

ISBN: 978-0-00-727422-2

Typeset in Sabon by Palimpsest Book Production Limited,
Grangemouth, Stirlingshire

Printed and bound in Great Britain by
Clays Ltd, St Ives plc

Mixed Sources
Product group from well-managed
forests and other controlled sources
www.fsc.org Cert no. SW-COC-1806
© 1996 Forest Stewardship Council

FSC is a non-profit international organisation established to promote the
responsible management of the world's forests. Products carrying the FSC
label are independently certified to assure consumers that they come
from forests that are managed to meet the social, economic and
ecological needs of present and future generations.

Find out more about HarperCollins and the environment at
www.harpercollins.co.uk/green

Publisher's Note

SAD WIND FROM THE SEA was first published in the UK by John Long in 1959 and later by Arrow in 1981. It was originally published under the name of Harry Patterson, an author who later became known to millions as Jack Higgins. This is the 50th anniversary edition of an amazing novel which has been out of print for some years, and in 2009, it seemed to the author and his publishers that it was a pity to leave such a good story languishing on his shelves. So we are delighted to be able to bring back SAD WIND FROM THE SEA for the pleasure of the vast majority of us who never had a chance to read the earlier editions.

For Amy

1

Macao 1953

When Hagen emerged from the gambling casino at the back of Charlie Beale's café he was drunk. He heard the door click into place behind him and for a moment he stood swaying as the cold night air cut into his lungs.

For several minutes he leaned against the wall, his forehead on the cool brickwork. After a while he pushed himself away and stood squarely, his feet braced firmly apart. He moved along the alley, taking slow, careful steps, and stood at the front of the café breathing deeply to clear his head. He fumbled in his pocket and found a crumpled packet of cigarettes. He lit one slowly and carefully and drew the smoke down into his lungs.

A thin sea-fog rolled in from the harbour, pushed by a cold finger of wind, and he coughed as it caught at the back of his throat. Except for the lapping of the water against the wharf pilings silence reigned. He wondered what time it was and instinctively lifted his right wrist and then remembered that his watch had followed the last of his money across the green baize top of one of Charlie Beale's tables. He decided it must be about three o'clock because he had that sort of feeling, or perhaps it was just that he was getting old. Too old for the kind of life he'd been living for the past four years. Too old to be making fortune depend on the turn of a card or the throw of the dice. He laughed suddenly as he considered his present position. His boat impounded by the Customs, his only means of livelihood cut off, and now the last of his money gone. You've really done it this time, he told himself. You've really excelled yourself. Somewhere a woman screamed.

He pushed himself from the wall and stood listening, head slightly forward. Again a scream sounded, curiously flat, and muffled by the fog.

Even as he told himself to mind his own business he was running. The liquor rolled heavily in his stomach and he cursed the poverty that forced him to drink cheap beer. He turned a corner, running silently on rope-soled feet, and took them by surprise. Two men were holding a struggling woman on the ground in the sickly yellow light of a street lamp.

As the nearest man turned in alarm, Hagen lifted a foot into his face and sent him spinning backwards over the edge of the wharf. The other leapt towards him, steel flickering in his right hand. In the brief moment of quiet as they circled each other Hagen saw that the man was Chinese and that murder shone from his eyes. He backed away as if frightened and the man grinned and rushed him. Hagen lifted an arm to ward off the knife-thrust and felt the sudden sharpness of pain even as he lifted his knee into his opponent's groin. The man writhed on the ground, an agony of twisting limbs, and Hagen coolly measured the distance and kicked him in the head.

There was quiet. He stood breathing deeply and looking down at the still form, wondering if he had killed him and not caring, and then he turned and searched for the woman. She was standing in the shadow of a warehouse door. He moved towards her and said, 'Are you all right?'

There was a faint movement of the white-clad figure and a soft voice said, 'Please stay where you are for a moment!' The voice surprised him and he wondered what an Englishwoman was doing on the waterfront of Macao at that time in the morning. There was more movement and then she stepped out of the shadows and came towards him. 'My dress was torn and I had to fix it,' she said.

He hardly heard what she was saying. She was only a girl, not more than seventeen or eighteen, and she was not English, although from the purity of her speech one of her parents must have been. Her skin had that creamy look peculiar to Eurasian women, and her lips an extra fullness that gave her a faintly sensual air. She had a breath-taking beauty of the kind that is always associated with simplicity. She stood before him looking gravely and steadily into his face and Hagen suddenly shivered for no accountable reason, as if somewhere someone had walked over his grave. He moistened dry lips and managed to speak. 'Where do you live?'

She mentioned the best hotel in Macao and he cursed silently, thinking of the walk that lay ahead of him. 'Can I get a taxi?' she asked in her clear, bell-like voice.

He laughed shortly. 'In this part of Macao, at this hour? You don't know this town, angel.'

She frowned and then her eyes widened and she reached forward and grabbed his arm. 'But you're hurt. There's blood on your sleeve!'

He smothered an oath as the sudden wrench caused a stab of pain to run through him. 'Take it easy,' he said and moved away to examine the wound under the light of the street lamp. His jacket had an ugly, blood-stained slit in it and when he wiped away the blood with a handkerchief he saw that he had sustained a superficial slash, more painful than anything else.

'How bad is it?' she asked him anxiously.

He shrugged. 'Not too bad. Hurts like hell, though.'

She took the handkerchief from his hand and twisted it neatly around his arm. 'Is that any better?' she said.

As he nodded he saw that her dress was badly torn. She'd made a pathetic attempt to pin it together, but it hardly measured up to the usual standards of decency. He made a sudden decision. 'There's only one way to get you back to your hotel,' he told her. 'We'll have to walk.' She nodded gravely and he added: 'We'd better call in at my hotel. You can fix this arm properly for me and I can get you a coat or something to cover yourself with.'

He nodded towards the bodice of her dress and she seemed to blush and instinctively put a hand there. 'That seems the best thing to do,' she said calmly. 'I think we'd better hurry, though. That handkerchief is proving an inadequate bandage.'

He was surprised at her calm acceptance of his suggestion. Surprised and also intrigued, because for a young girl who had just been through a pretty bad experience she seemed remarkably unaffected. His hotel was only a quarter of a mile away and as they approached it he suddenly felt uncomfortable. As he held the door open for her he reflected bitterly that the place looked what it was – a flea-bag. A blast of hot, stale air met them from the small hall and an ancient fan creaked, slowly and uselessly, above their heads, hardly causing a movement in the air.

The Chinese night-clerk was asleep at his desk, his head between his hands, and Hagen motioned the girl to silence. It didn't work. Half-way across the hall a polite cough sounded behind them and Hagen turned wearily. The night-clerk, now fully awake, smiled in an apologetic manner. Hagen felt in his pocket and then remembered that he was broke. 'Have you got a petaka?' he asked the girl. She frowned and looked puzzled. 'I'm broke, flat, and I need a petaka.' He gestured helpfully at the fly-blown sign on the wall: NO FEMALES ALLOWED UPSTAIRS. He grinned tiredly as she turned from reading the notice.

'They much prefer to supply their own, you see!' This time he had her in a better light and she did blush. She fumbled in her handbag and gave him a Straits dollar. He flipped it to the clerk and they mounted the rickety stairs.

He felt even more ashamed of his room than he had done about the hotel. It looked like a pigsty and smelled like one. Empty gin bottles in one corner and soiled clothing in another, combined with an unmade bed, did not make a very savoury picture. The girl didn't seem to notice. 'Have you got any bandages?' she demanded.

He rummaged about under the bed and finally produced the first-aid kit he had salvaged from the boat, and she led the way into the bathroom and told him to strip to the waist.

She carefully washed the congealed blood away and frowned. 'This should be stitched.'

He shook his head. 'I heal quickly.'

She smiled and pointed to the numerous scars on his chest and stomach. 'You must do.'

He grinned. 'Souvenir of the war. Shrapnel. Looks worse than it was.'

She carefully bandaged his arm and said, 'Which war – Korea?'

He shook his head. 'No, my war was a long time ago, angel. A thousand years ago.' She pressed surgical tape across the loose ends of the bandage and looked quickly up into his face. The sharp triangle that formed his chin was covered with a dark stubble that accentuated the hollowness of his cheeks and the dark sombreness of the eyes. For a brief moment he looked down at her and then he said, 'You've done this sort of thing before,' and gestured to his bandaged arm.

She nodded. 'A little – but even that was too much.'

Suddenly she began to shiver uncontrollably and Hagen slipped his arm about her shoulders and squeezed. 'You're all right,' he told her. 'It's all over.' She nodded several times and broke away from him, and stood over by the window, her back towards him. He opened a drawer and by a miracle discovered a clean shirt. By the time he was properly dressed again she had recovered.

'That was rather silly of me,' she said. 'The

essential feminine weakness coming out, I suppose.'

Hagen laughed. 'What you need is a drink.' He poured gin into two moderately clean glasses and, crossing the room, kicked open the window and led the way out on to the balcony. The girl sat in the only chair and Hagen leaned on the balcony rail and for a short time there was silence.

'Do you think I might have a cigarette?' Her voice spoke gently from the darkness. He fumbled in his pocket and finally discovered the battered packet. As the match flared in his cupped hands, and she leaned forward, the delicate beauty of her face was thrown into relief. He held the match for a moment longer than was necessary, and they looked briefly into each other's eyes, and then he flicked the match out into the darkness in a long, curving arc. 'I'd like to thank you for what you did back there.' She spoke slowly and carefully as though searching for words.

'Girls like you shouldn't be on the water-front in the early hours,' he told her.

As if she had suddenly arrived at a decision

her voice sounded again from the darkness, this time more assured and confident. 'My name is Rose Graham.'

So he had been right about one of her parents, at least. He half-turned towards her. 'Mark Hagen. Captain Hagen I'm known as in these parts.'

'Oh, you are a sea captain?'

'I have a small boat,' he told her. It came to him that he was wrong. The operative word was 'had'. I had a small boat, he thought. What have I got now? Another thought struck him, more immediate, more urgent. 'Was I in time back there?' he said. 'I mean, did those mugs really harm you or anything?' He felt suddenly awkward.

The chair creaked as she stood up. 'They didn't harm me, Captain Hagen. It wasn't that kind of an assault.'

She moved to the rail and stood beside him so that his shoulder touched hers lightly each time he stirred. The wind blew in from the sea and the mist rolled across the harbour, and the riding lights of the ships glowed faintly through the gaps that appeared every so often when the wind tore a hole in the grey curtain. From the balcony the view was magnificent and suddenly Hagen felt at peace and restless, happy and discontented, all at the same time. It had been a bad day and the past came too easily to mind. He decided that it was all the girl's fault. It had been a long time since he had been so close to someone like her. He sighed and straightened up.

She laughed lightly. 'What are you thinking about? It must be something pretty sad to make you sigh so heavily.'

He grinned and took out another cigarette. 'I was contemplating a misspent life, angel,' he told her. 'I seem to be making a habit of it lately. I must be getting old.'

She laughed again. 'How ridiculous. You aren't old. You're still a young man.'

'I'm thirty-five,' he said. 'When you've lived the life I have, then believe me – it's old.' A thought came to him and he smiled to himself and added, 'How old are you, anyway?'

She said eighteen, in a small voice. Hagen laughed. 'There you are. I'm twice your age.

I'm old enough to be your father. In fact I'd say it's about time you were safely tucked up in bed.'

He walked back into the bedroom and started to put on his jacket. She followed at his heels and stood watching him, playing nervously with the silk scarf that was twisted round her throat. She spoke in a high-pitched voice. 'I don't think it would be very wise for you to see me back to my hotel.'

He straightened up slowly and looked at her without speaking. She flushed and dropped her eyes and he said, 'If you think I'm going to let you walk two miles through the worst part of Macao on your own, you're crazy.'

She darted past him and had the door half open before his hand gripped her arm and pulled her back. She struggled for a moment and then relaxed suddenly and completely and said despairingly, 'Captain Hagen, I'm trying to tell you that if you take me back to my hotel you may be involving yourself in more ways than you think.'

Hagen took a crumpled linen jacket from behind the door and handed it to her. 'Here, woman! Cover thy nakedness!' He intoned the words with deliberate pomposity.

She dissolved into laughter and for a moment or two they laughed together. When she spoke again the edge of nervousness had gone, but she was still desperately serious when she said: 'You've been very kind to me. It's just that I don't want to see you get mixed up in something that isn't your concern.'

'I suppose this all ties in with your being on the waterfront at such a peculiar hour?'

She nodded. 'I had to see a friend. He telephoned and asked me to meet him at a certain warehouse. The taxi-driver wouldn't wait and then those men . . .'

'I still think it was a funny hour to see a friend and if he knows this town he shouldn't have asked you to come to a quarter like this at such a time.' Hagen was surprised to discover that he really felt angry about the whole thing. 'If I hadn't arrived you'd probably have ended up in the harbour.'

She turned away, desperation on her face again. 'But don't you see,' she said, 'it wasn't that kind of an assault. Those men wanted some information and they'll try again. If you are seen with me . . .'

She left the sentence unfinished and shrugged her shoulders. Hagen considered the point for a moment and then he went over to his bed and felt under the pillow. When he straightened up he was holding an American service issue Colt automatic. He checked the action of the weapon and slipped it into his pocket. He grinned and, opening the door, motioned her out. 'I love trouble, angel,' he said. 'It makes life so much more exciting.' For a brief moment she stared at him and then her face relaxed into a smile and she went through the door without a word.

It took about forty minutes to reach her hotel. The girl hardly spoke a word on the way. Hagen guessed that she was almost on the point of collapse and finally slipped a hand under her arm. She leaned heavily on him and a faint, delicate perfume tingled in his nostrils. For a moment he savoured its sweetness pleasantly and then impatiently shrugged it aside and concentrated on keeping alert in case of trouble.

At the foot of the steps leading up to her hotel they halted. Hagen said, 'Well, this is it.'

She nodded sleepily. 'Will I see you again?'

For a moment he considered the question and doubts raced through his mind. The girl meant trouble – big trouble. He was sure of that and he had enough troubles of his own at the moment. He made his decision suddenly as she swayed forward tiredly and bumped against him. 'Yes, you'll see me again, angel,' he said. 'I'll drop in around noon.'

He smiled reassuringly and patted her on the shoulder. 'Noon,' she said and suddenly warmed into life. A deep smile bloomed on her face. She reached up and pulling down his head, kissed him lightly on the mouth, and then turned and ran up the steps and into the hotel.

For a moment Hagen stood there, her fragrance still with him, then he turned away and began to walk briskly back towards the waterfront. He smoked a cigarette and thought about her and now and then a tiny smile tugged at the corners of his mouth. As if he didn't have enough trouble. 'You never learn,' he said, half-aloud, and as he bent his head to sniff again at the fragrance on his shoulder where her head had rested, a bullet dunted the wall beside him.

As he ran for the shelter of a warehouse doorway, a car engine started up, and a large limousine appeared through the fog like a menacing monster and hurtled towards him. Hagen scrambled into the safety of the doorway and, turning, pulled out his automatic and loosed three shots in rapid succession at the car. It swerved wildly and scraped a fender as it rounded the corner of the street and disappeared. The whole thing had happened in a matter of seconds. Only the reflex action of several years of hard living had saved him.

He kept to the wall for the rest of the way to his hotel and held the automatic at the ready, but nothing happened. When he entered the hall the night-clerk was still asleep, head propped between his hands. Hagen had reached the foot of the stairs before a thought struck him. He turned back to the desk and shook the sleeping man by the shoulder. It was several moments before he awakened. Hagen was intrigued. Only a short time before the man had been awakened by the faint sounds made by two people quietly crossing the hall. Now it took several moments of hard shaking to wake him. The man raised his head and looked at him in surprise and said politely: 'Ah, Captain Hagen. You are back.'

Hagen leaned on the desk and said casually, 'Has anyone been asking for me?'

'At this time in the morning?' The clerk was trying to sound surprised and failing badly. 'You joke me?'

Hagen lifted the flap and was on the other side of the desk in one smooth movement. 'No, I don't joke you,' he said and grabbed the terrified man by the lapels. 'Now start talking. Who enquired after me?'

'No! Please. I have nothing to say.'

Hagen produced the automatic. 'That's a pity,' he said, 'because you've got about ten seconds to change your mind before I start wiping this across your face.'

He chucked the man under the chin with

the barrel by way of encouragement and the clerk cried out suddenly. 'I talk! I talk!' His voice was cracked and high-pitched like an old woman's and he was sweating with fear. 'Just after you and lady leave, two men come in. Very nasty, very rough. They ask about you. One have knife. He say I not talk, they cut my throat. What I do? I tell what they want to know and they leave.'

The sing-song voice finished mangling the English language and he stood shaking like a frightened little bird looking for some place to hide. Hagen thought for a moment and said, 'Were these men white men?'

'No! They Chinese.'

Hagen nodded. 'Do you know them? Have you ever seen them around here before?'

The night-clerk's eyes dropped and he looked more afraid than ever. 'Not from Macao. Me think they from mainland.'

Hagen left him there, frightened and whimpering, and went slowly upstairs. He took all the time in the world to enter his room. He kicked open the door and went in at ground level with the automatic at the ready, but there was no one there. He poured himself a drink and lay on the bed in the dark, smoking and thinking about the whole affair. Men from the mainland. So the Commies were mixed up in this thing, were they? He felt sorry for Rose Graham. It didn't pay to cross those people. He'd had dealings with them before. Anyway, why was he worrying about the girl so much? He had his own worries. Getting his boat back was the only thing that mattered at the moment. To hell with her. He'd saved her life. That was enough.

He stubbed out his cigarette and lay back and as sleep pulled its dark cloak over him, he chuckled quietly, because he knew damned well that he would keep the appointment at noon. He seemed to feel her lips pressed against his and his last conscious thought was of her face glowing in the darkness and she was smiling at him.

2

Noon of that day found Hagen entering the swing door of her hotel. He was immaculately dressed in a white shark-skin suit, specially pressed for the occasion. He crossed the spacious lounge to the desk and the receptionist, an aristocratic-looking White Russian, glanced up from a letter he was reading. His eyes flickered over the expensive suit and a smile appeared on his mouth. 'Good morning, sir. What can I do for you?'

Hagen asked for the girl and there was an immediate drop in the temperature. The smile was replaced by a slight frown and the Russian told him coldly that she was in, but that it was a rule of the hotel that visitors

must first be announced on the internal telephone before proceeding upstairs. He lifted
the receiver and asked to be put through to
her room. Anger and instinctive dislike stirred
in Hagen. He waited until the man had Rose
Graham on the phone and then reached
across and twisted the receiver from his grasp.
The Russian stalked away, an outraged
expression on his face. Hagen turned his back
and said: 'Hello, angel! Did you sleep well?'

Her voice sounded clear and sweet as a
ship's bell across water. 'Captain Hagen! But
I've only just awakened.'

He laughed pleasantly. 'As you've obviously
missed breakfast, how about having lunch
with me?' He fingered the few notes he had
in his pocket, his final reserve, and she asked
him to give her twenty minutes to shower
and dress.

Hagen sat in one of the numerous easy
chairs and leafed through a month-old
American magazine. He was only half-
interested, however, and most of the time he
found himself thinking about the girl and
waiting with anticipation for the moment

when she would join him. It was a new feeling. A disturbing feeling. He hadn't been so interested in a woman for a long time. There was something ingenuous and refreshing about her. She had accepted his lunch invitation with a delight that she had not attempted to conceal and he wondered, suddenly, if he was getting involved in something serious. He dismissed the idea from his mind with a shrug. This would be their last meeting. Lunch for two to round the whole affair off. He beckoned to a passing waiter and ordered a gin-sling. As the drink was brought to him he noticed the Russian receptionist sneering at him from the desk and instinctively Hagen tossed the waiter a large tip. The Russian's sneer vanished rapidly. He must have imagined he was now on bad terms with a tipping customer. Hagen sipped his drink and sighed. A few more grand gestures and he really would be broke.

He glanced idly across at the lift doors as they opened and the girl stepped out. He stood up and walked towards her and she looked eagerly around and then she saw him and a warm smile appeared on her face. She came towards him and as she passed the reception desk a voice said: 'Oh, Miss Graham. Have you a moment?'

It was the Russian who had spoken. Hagen stood, hat in hand, a few feet away and feigned an interest in some travel brochures. He tried to pick up as much of the conversation as he could. The gist of it seemed to be that she hadn't paid her hotel bill for three weeks and the Russian wasn't being too polite about telling her. Hagen half-turned towards them, wondering whether he should intervene, when the girl opened her handbag and took out a cheque-book. She scribbled furiously for a moment, tore out the cheque, and flung it into the Russian's face.

She turned to Hagen and cursed the man fluently in Malay, Cantonese and a dialect that was new to him. 'They think because I am a Eurasian they can treat me any way they like, these people.'

Hagen smiled. 'The cheque act was the best part of the show,' he told her.

She smiled up at him, a tight little smile,

and suddenly her face seemed to crumple and she began to cry. Before they could attract any attention Hagen gripped her arm and rushed her into the American Bar. Everyone had gone to lunch and for the moment the bar was cool, dark and empty. He left her in a booth to get the crying fit over and went and sat on one of the high stools at the bar and had a whisky-and-water.

He was puzzled. The girl was well educated and her clothes were expensive. She was obviously used to the best. One didn't usually leave hotel bills unpaid for three weeks when one had a cheque-book. He began to wonder just how much was left in that bank account. He even wondered whether the cheque she had just written would bounce right back into the Russian receptionist's face. It was a pleasant thought. The girl moved on to a stool beside him. She had fixed her face so that only an unnatural brightness in the eyes indicated that she had been crying. 'Could I have a drink, please?'

'Surely! A gin-sling?' She nodded and he ordered the drink. He didn't speak until the barman had placed the drink before her and retired to the other end of the bar to polish glasses. 'Can you meet that cheque?'

She smiled wanly and sipped her drink. 'Only just. A few dollars left and then . . .' She shrugged her shoulders; a hopeless gesture that seemed to say she was at the end of her tether. This was the moment for the gallant gesture, Hagen thought. It suddenly occurred to him how ironic it was that of all the people in Macao she should have met him and he laughed aloud. She flushed angrily. 'What's so funny?' she demanded.

He hastened to reassure her. 'I'm not laughing at *you*, angel. It's just that I'm in a pretty poor state myself at the moment. We make a nice pair.' She began to laugh herself and Hagen remembered that he still had a little money left. Suddenly he felt reckless and past caring. He grabbed her arm and propelled her firmly out of the bar. 'There's one thing we can do,' he said. 'And that's to have lunch. Things always look brighter after a decent meal.'

He kept up a running flow of conversation

on the way to the dining-room and by the time they were seated at a table there was a smile on her face again. During the meal they talked little. She had a healthy appetite and he found himself covertly watching her at every opportunity. Once or twice she noticed his eyes and blushed. 'That was lovely,' she said at length. 'I couldn't eat another bite.'

Hagen suggested a drink on the terrace and ordered a couple of brandies before following her out there. She was seated at a table on the very edge of the terrace. Below them was Macao and the view stretched across the blue water to Kowloon and the Chinese mainland. 'It's beautiful,' he said, and offered her a cigarette.

She nodded and refused the cigarette. 'It's a lovely city. Very lovely.' She paused as the waiter brought the drinks and Hagen suddenly sensed that she was on the verge of telling him about herself.

She still hesitated and he said, quickly, 'Have you been here long?'

She shook her head. 'Only the three weeks that I've been staying at the hotel.' She gazed out over the harbour. 'I should have found somewhere cheaper I suppose, but a girl on her own! It's very difficult.'

Hagen reached across the table and placed his hand gently over hers. 'Why don't you tell me about it?' he said softly. 'I know it's something to do with our Red friends across the water.'

She straightened up, fear on her face. 'How do you know?'

He explained briefly. 'So you see,' he concluded, 'I'm mixed up in this thing enough to get shot at. The least you can do is tell me what it's all about.'

For a little while she stared at the table, her fingers nervously interlacing, and then she began to speak. 'I'm from Indo-China – the North. My father was a Scot. Mother was Indo-Chinese. I went to school in India, spent the war there. Afterwards I returned to my father's plantation. He'd been on some special service during the war, in Malaya. Things were just beginning to settle down again when the trouble started between the French and the Viet Minh.'

Hagen nodded. 'That must have messed things up pretty badly. Especially as you were living in the North.'

'Yes, things couldn't have been worse. It wasn't long before we were completely surrounded by Communist territory. At first they didn't bother us, but then one day . . .'

For a moment she seemed to have difficulty in finding words. She turned her head away a little and Hagen reached across again and took her hand firmly. 'Go on, angel. Get rid of it.'

She smiled tightly. 'My mother. They killed my mother. Father and I had been out for the day. We got home just as three Communist soldiers were leaving. My father had an automatic rifle. He shot them.' She gazed away out over the water, into the past. 'He did it very expertly. He must have had quite a hard war.'

'Finish your drink,' Hagen told her. 'Brandy is the best pick-me-up I know.'

She gulped the brandy too fast, choked and made a wry face. After a moment she continued. 'Dad couldn't forgive himself for not getting us out sooner. You see he'd been preparing for quite some time. He had a thirty-foot launch hidden in a nearby creek and we were going to go down-river to the coast and then south to Hanoi.'

'Why had he delayed so long?' Hagen demanded.

She traced a delicate pattern with a finger in a pool of spilled brandy. 'Because he'd promised to take something with him and it wasn't ready.'

Hagen swallowed some of his brandy and said, 'Was it all that important?'

'If you'd call a quarter of a million dollars important,' she said calmly.

Hagen finished his brandy and put the glass down very carefully. 'How much did you say?'

She smiled. 'I'm not exaggerating. A quarter of a million – in gold. There was a Buddhist monastery near the plantation. The gold was theirs. They knew that sooner or later the Communists would arrive to loot the place. They decided that they'd rather see their treasure doing good in the hands of some relief organization than swelling the war chest of Ho Chi-minh.'

'Did you say in gold, angel?' Hagen asked.

She nodded. 'Gold bars. That's what caused the delay. They melted down some statues. It was the only safe way of transporting the stuff.'

'What happened?' Hagen demanded. 'What did your father do with it?'

She fiddled with her glass for a little while. 'Oh, he had it loaded into the cabin in boxes and we set off. There were just three of us. The deck-hand was our Malayan house-boy, Tewak. We reached the coast and ran into a gunboat. There was a fight. I remember my father ramming the other boat and throwing a hand grenade. I don't know, really. It's difficult to recall these things clearly. It was confused – and besides, he was badly hit.' She brooded for a moment and then looked up suddenly. 'Do you know the Kwai Marshes, just over the border from Viet Minh into China?'

Hagen nodded. 'I know it. It's a pest hole. Hundreds of miles of channels and reeds, lagoons and swamp. Rotten with disease.'

She nodded. 'That's the place. That's where Dad took the boat. She was leaking badly. He ran her into the Kwai Marshes. She sank in a little lagoon surrounded by reeds.' Hagen waited for the end. She sat back suddenly and said briskly: 'After that it was simple. My father died the next day. It took Tewak and me three days to get out of the marshes. We went down the coast to Haiphong and from there to Saigon. Luckily I had a little money in a bank there.'

'What about the gold?' Hagen said. 'You told the French authorities, I suppose?'

'Oh, yes,' she said. 'I told the French. They weren't interested in sending an expedition into Communist China to retrieve a mere quarter of a million dollars. It wouldn't keep the war going for ten minutes.'

'I see,' Hagen said carefully. 'So the gold is still there?'

She nodded. 'Still there. I've tried to get a boat to take me back to the marshes. At first people were too scared to take the risk. Now, I've not got enough money to pay. That's why we came to Macao.'

'We?' Hagen said.

She explained. 'Tewak. He's stayed with me the whole time. He has friends in Macao. We came here because it was our last hope. He's been trying to borrow a boat for the past three weeks.'

Light suddenly dawned on Hagen. 'It was Tewak who rang you last night?'

She nodded. 'That's right. He asked me to get a taxi at once and meet him where you found me. When I got there he wasn't to be seen. After the taxi had left those two men appeared.'

Hagen said, 'It looks as though the Reds don't intend to let that gold slip through their fingers.'

'Not if I can help it,' she said, and for a moment her face was cold and hard.

'You know the position where the boat sank?' Hagen asked, casually.

'Oh, yes,' she told him. 'I memorized it. One could search for ever in those marshes without it.'

Hagen stood up and leaned on the parapet, and stared out over the water into the far distance. His eyes didn't see the ships in the bay or the ferry from Kowloon as it ploughed its way towards Macao. They saw a quiet lagoon surrounded by giant marsh reeds and a thirty-foot launch lying in clear water, and the boxes in the cabin that contained the discoloured gold bars. A quarter of a million dollars. His palms were sweating slightly and his mouth had gone dry. It could be the one stroke a man dreamed of. The big deal. No more waterfront hotels in stinking, godforsaken ports. No more smuggling and gun-running, being betrayed and twisted and double-crossed at every turn. If he could lay hands on that gold he could be set for life. He turned back to the table and she looked at him sadly. 'Cheer up, angel,' he said. 'Things have been pretty rough but they'll get better. Just wait until you've got your hands on all that loot. You'll be able to live like a princess.'

She looked puzzled for a moment and then understanding came and she hastened to correct him. 'The money for the sale of the gold is not for me.' Hagen sat bolt upright in his chair. 'I'll only get a little for expenses. The rest goes to the relief organization in Saigon just as the monks and my father wanted.'

She was absolutely sincere in what she had just said. She really meant to give all that money to some crackpot relief organization. For a moment Hagen was tempted to tell her the facts of life, but that could wait until later. 'How deep was that lagoon, angel?' he said.

She looked surprised. 'I couldn't be sure but not very deep. Perhaps twenty or twenty-five feet. Why do you ask?'

He shrugged and lit a cigarette carefully. 'I have a boat. I've done some pearling. I've also been to the Kwai Marshes.'

She gazed at him searchingly for a moment. 'You mean you would be willing to take me to the Kwai?' She frowned. 'But why?' He gazed at her steadily, hating himself, and suddenly she gave a little, breathless laugh. 'I see, I . . .' She was lost in her confusion and colour flooded her face.

Hagen squeezed her hand and firmly

pushed every other consideration from his mind. He must think only of the gold. After all, it wouldn't be too hard to pretend that he loved her. 'I'd better be honest with you from the beginning,' he said. 'And then there won't be misunderstandings or hurt. I'm known pretty well round these parts and not for the best of reasons. I'm a smuggler, gun-runner, illegal pearler. In fact, anything that pays.' She nodded slowly and he went on: 'At the moment my boat is in the hands of the Portuguese Customs. The funny thing is that for once I was genuinely innocent.' For a moment he thought about 'Inter-Island Trading Incorporated' and his sleeping partner, Mr Papoudopulous. Beware of Greeks bearing gifts. Still, it was all in the game. He smiled sardonically at the girl and went on: 'They found gold under the cabin floor. I was fined rather heavily. In fact, I didn't have the money, so – they impounded the boat.'

'Can you get the money?' she said.

He nodded. 'Yes, I can borrow it from a friend, but you'll have to agree to the payment of my expenses and the loan from the proceeds of the sale of the gold.'

She nodded eagerly. 'Oh, yes. That will be fine. It will be well worth it.' A puzzled frown creased her brow and she leaned across the table. 'Mark, all those things you did. Why? I don't understand. You don't seem to be that kind of a man.'

He realized dispassionately that she had used his Christian name and that it had never sounded quite so well before. He grinned. 'It's a long and sordid story, angel. One of these days I might tell it to you, but for the moment there are more important things to consider. Tewak, for instance. I'd like to know what happened to him last night. Are you sure it was his voice on the telephone?'

She nodded emphatically. 'He had a lisp. No one could have simulated it in quite the same way.'

Hagen decided that it didn't look so good for Tewak. The story was beginning to take shape. The Commies had traced the girl all the way from the Kwai to Macao. They had agents in every Eastern city and it must have been pretty simple. It was natural they should go to so much trouble. After all, the gold was actually in their own territory. He decided that either Tewak had been forced to make that telephone call or, alternatively, had been known to make it and had been dealt with afterwards.

'What's the next move?' Rose said.

Hagen snapped a finger at the waiter and put most of his remaining money on the table. 'The next move, angel, will be a quick call at my hotel. From now on I don't intend to take a step without that Colt automatic.'

They left the hotel and took a taxi down to the waterfront. Hagen left Rose in the cab and ran up to his room for the automatic. As they completed the journey to the address she had given the driver Hagen checked the automatic and reloaded the clip. Rose shuddered. 'I hate guns,' she said. 'I hate them.'

He patted her hand. 'Next to the dog they're a man's most faithful friend.' The cab stopped with a jolt in a deserted street and he handed her out and paid the man off.

He recognized the building. It was a seedy

tenement used as a hotel by coloured seamen. It wasn't the sort of establishment that kept a receptionist. They entered a dark and gloomy hall and before them stretched a flight of dangerous-looking wooden stairs. Hagen groped his way upwards and Rose followed behind, gripping his belt. The smell was appalling and a brooding quiet hung over the place. Hagen held the automatic in his right hand against his thigh and, with his left, held a flickering match, by which light he attempted to read the numbers on the room doors. Number eighteen was the last door in the corridor on the left-hand side and it swung open to his touch.

The room was in darkness. He paused for a moment and listened. There was utter silence everywhere. He decided to risk it and struck a match. There was a man sitting in a chair in the centre of the room. His hands were bound behind him and he was completely naked. Hagen gazed in fascinated horror at the scores of cuts and slashes that covered the body, and then his gaze travelled lower down and he shuddered with disgust as he saw what had been done. He heard Rose move into the room behind him and even as he turned to warn her to stay out she cried, 'Tewak!', and then she screamed. At that moment the match burned Hagen's finger-tips and he hurriedly dropped it, plunging the room into darkness again.

The girl sagged against him, half-fainting, and he quickly walked her from the room. He stood in the hall holding her close to him for a minute and then said, 'Are you all right?'

She straightened up. 'Yes, I'll be fine. Really I will. It was just the shock.'

'Good girl.' He handed her the automatic. 'You know how this thing works, I suppose. The safety is off. If anyone comes near you just pull the trigger. I'll only be a short while, I promise.'

He went back into the room and closed the door behind him. He struck another match and the light was reflected in grue-some fashion from the eyes of the dead man which had turned up so that only the whites were visible. Hagen moved to the window and tore down the blanket that had been improvised as a curtain. He began to examine the room. It was not pleasant moving around with that macabre horror sitting in the centre, but he had to see if anything of interest had been left.

The room was devoid of furniture except for an old iron bedstead and the chair. There was a cupboard but it contained only a few odds and ends of clothes left there by previous occupants. Hagen finally steeled himself to examine the body closely. In any Western country the murder would have been considered the work of a lunatic, but Hagen, familiar with the Oriental mind and its refinements in cruelty and contempt for human life, drew no such conclusion. The men who had done this thing had wanted information badly. Torture was to them the obvious key to a stubborn tongue. The final mutilation looked as though it had been committed in a fit of rage after death. Hagen decided that Tewak had probably refused to talk. Sweat stung his eyes and as he wiped it away he realized why the building was so unnaturally quiet. With their usual sixth sense for trouble he knew there wouldn't be a single seaman left in the place. He opened the door with a final glance round and stepped outside.

The girl tried to smile but only succeeded in looking sick. Hagen took the gun from her and slipped it into his pocket. 'You need a drink,' he said and, taking her by the arm, he hurried her from the building.

He took her to a little bar he knew nearby and they sat in the privacy of a booth cut off from the noisy world by a bead curtain. He lit a cigarette and put it into her mouth. She inhaled two or three times and seemed to be a little better. 'I'm sorry,' she said. 'It was the most horrible thing I've ever seen.' She shuddered.

The drinks came at that moment and Hagen pushed hers across. 'Drink up,' he said. 'It'll do you good. I'm not exactly soft myself but it's one of the worst things I've ever seen.'

She smiled tightly. 'You seem to have done nothing but rush me into quiet bars while I cry,' she said. He smiled and gripped her hand tightly. 'What am I going to do?' she moaned.

'Do you still want to go after that gold?' he demanded. She nodded. 'Then that's settled. Now, the best thing for you this afternoon would be to go back to your hotel and lie down.' She started to protest. 'No buts,' Hagen added. 'I'm in command. Anyway, I've got a lot to arrange and you'd only be in the way.'

They left the bar and he hailed a taxi. When he paid it off at the hotel he was left almost penniless. He was going to leave her at the entrance but she begged him to come up for just a moment. The lift took them to the third floor. Her room was at the end of the corridor and she gave him the key. When he opened the door the room was a shambles. Clothing and personal effects were strewn about the place and most of the drawers had been taken out completely. 'But why?' she said. 'What did they expect to find?'

Hagen pushed his hat back from his forehead. 'The directions for finding the launch, angel. They were hoping you might be stupid enough to leave them lying around.'

'The fools,' she exploded. 'What do they take me for? I know the position by heart.'

Hagen said in a satisfied tone: 'One thing it proves. Tewak didn't talk.' Suddenly Rose began to curse in the same fluent manner in which she had blasted the Russian clerk. 'Heh, hold on,' Hagen said.

'Oh, damn them!' she said. 'I'm beginning to get annoyed.'

'No tears?' he said.

'They're all used up.'

He grinned and took off his jacket. 'Let's get started packing your things.'

'Why the hurry?' she said in surprise.

'You can't stay here. I think I'd better take you to visit a friend of mine.'

She shrugged her shoulders and started to pack the things in her cases as he handed them to her. Within twenty minutes they were leaving the room preceded by a couple of boys carrying the luggage. The Russian was scrupulously polite and remote when making out the bill. As they turned away from the desk Hagen suddenly shouted, 'Here, boy!' and tossed a coin which the man instinctively caught. He stood glaring after them in fury and several people laughed. Hagen decided that the coin had been worth it.

As the taxi headed up into the residential part of Macao on the hill, Rose said curiously, 'What is this friend of yours like?'

Hagen said casually, 'All right, I think you'll like her.'

'Oh, a woman.' There was a faint edge to her words. 'An old friend?'

He laughed. 'Yes, in both senses of the phrase.' He patted her hand. 'Don't worry. She's very well known. All the best people go to her house. All the best men do, anyway.'

It took several moments for the implication of his words to sink in. Rose gasped. 'You don't mean she keeps . . .' – she fumbled for words – 'a house!'

'She certainly does,' Hagen said. 'The best

house in Macao.' Even as he spoke and Rose sank back in her seat, crimson with embarrassment, the taxi turned into a side road and braked to a halt outside a pair of beautiful and intricate wrought-iron gates set in a high stone wall.

3

Hagen told the taxi-driver to wait, and he and the girl walked up to the ornate iron gates. He pulled on a bellrope and after a while a huge, misshapen figured shambled up to the other side of the gates. A flat, Mongolian face was pressed against the iron-work as the owner peered short-sightedly at them. Hagen reached through and pulled the man's nose. 'What the hell, Lee,' he said. 'Don't you remember old friends?'

The face split into a grin and the gate was hurriedly unlocked. As they passed through Hagen punched him lightly in his massive chest and said, 'Bring the luggage in when I tell you,

Lee.' The Mongolian nodded vigorously, his smile fixed firmly in position.

As they walked up the drive towards the imposing-looking house, Rose said: 'He's so grotesque, like an ape Why doesn't he speak?'

Hagen laughed. 'The Japs cut out his tongue. He's the bouncer here. He could break the back of any man I ever knew.' She appeared suitably impressed and he added: 'Just remember, angel. If you stay here that so-called ape will protect you when I'm not around. Maybe that thought will make him look a little prettier.'

A maid admitted them with a smile of welcome for Hagen, and showed them into a large reception room. Rose was fascinated by the incredible luxury of the room. There seemed to be a small fortune in Chinese *objets d'art*. Somewhere nearby a loud voice could be heard and then the door was kicked open and the most fantastic-looking woman Rose had ever seen stormed into the room. 'Mark Hagen – you young hellion.' Her voice was like a foghorn and she swept across the floor and crushed him in her arms.

She was wearing a gold kimono and black lounging pyjamas, and the colour scheme clashed terribly with vivid red-dyed hair. 'Clara, do you still love me?' Hagen demanded.

'No one else, handsome.' She kissed him enthusiastically on one cheek, leaving a smear of vivid orange, and turned and boldly regarded the girl.

Hagen said: 'Rose, I'd like you to meet Clara Boydell. Clara, this is Rose Graham.'

Clara reached for a silver box and offered him a cheroot and took one herself. 'My God, Mark,' she said, 'I wish I could find a few like her. I'd make a fortune.'

Rose coloured and dropped her eyes and Hagen said, 'Look, Clara, I need a big favour.'

Clara flung herself down in an easy chair that protested loudly at her weight. 'Anything I can do. I owe you a favour or two.' She straightened up and added, 'Anything except money, that is.' She turned and explained to Rose: 'One thing I never do, honey, is part with cash. I need it all for my old age.'

'It isn't money, Clara,' Hagen said. 'I'd like

you to put Rose up for a few days. There are a few people she wants to avoid in town.'

The woman looked at him through narrowed eyes for a moment or two and then she smiled. 'Sure, why not?' She rang a handbell. 'It won't cost me anything.'

Hagen grinned. 'There's just one thing, Clara. I've a taxi waiting at the gates with the luggage. I'm afraid I'm flat.'

She scowled at him ferociously and then, as the maid came in, her face broke into a smile. 'Okay, handsome. Just this once.' She gave the maid an order in execrable Cantonese and said to Rose: 'Go with her, honey. She'll fix you up in one of the guest-rooms.'

Rose smiled her thanks and as she went out of the door Hagen said, 'I'll see you later, angel.'

'And I'll see *you* now,' Clara Boydell said. Hagen closed the door and turned towards her. She poured two generous measures of gin into glasses and said: 'Okay, Mark. Tell me what you're mixed up in this time.'

Hagen dropped into an easy chair and relaxed. He was more tired than he had realized. Over the top of his glass he regarded Clara Boydell. In the past they had served each other too well for mistrust to enter into their relationship at this stage. He knew that this woman had a genuine affection for him. He told her most of what had happened and what he intended to do.

When he had finished she sat silently staring out of the window. She looked serious and he had never known her to be serious in the four years they had been friends. 'Well, what do you think?' he said.

'I think the whole thing stinks.'

He jumped up and restlessly paced back and forth across the room. 'What the hell, Clara. I know it's risky but you don't get anything easily in this world.'

'I'm not just thinking of the risks,' she told him. 'I like the look of that kid and you're going to swindle her.'

'For God's sake,' he said angrily. 'I'm not throwing the kid to the sharks. I'll see that she gets a cut.'

'Who says she'll want a cut and, anyway, she's in love with you.'

Hagen laughed shortly. 'Don't be a fool. I only met her a few hours ago.'

'Yes, and saved her life. She was in a spot and you came along and pulled her out of it and since then you've taken charge of things for her. If she doesn't love you at the moment she soon will do.' Hagen snorted and poured himself another drink and Clara continued: 'Don't be a fool, Mark. Forget about the girl and look at it from the other angle. If you go into those marshes the Commies will never let you come out alive. They'll be watching every move you make. They may let you in. They may even let you do all the work, but in the end they'll strike. It's suicide, Mark. Are you that desperate for money?'

Hagen walked to the window and spoke without turning round. 'Clara, I'm sick of the life I've been leading. I've had enough. The years are rolling by and what have I got to show? Nothing. I want to go home with my pockets full before it's too late. Is that a bad thing to want?' He turned and looked at her and she shrugged helplessly. 'All right,' he said, 'I'll put it plainly. If I don't take this chance I'm all washed up. Just another bum on the beach. Maybe I will get killed – so what? I'd rather take the risk. If I don't get the gold I'm better off dead anyway.'

He walked over to the door and opened it. 'Okay, Mark,' she said. 'Have it your own way.'

He smiled sadly. 'I intend to, Clara. Tell Rose I'll be back to see her this evening, will you?' She nodded and he closed the door gently behind him.

He had hoped at the back of his mind that Clara, properly approached, might be willing to finance the deal for him. That hope was dead now and he directed his steps towards the centre of Macao to start the rounds of the bankers and money-lenders. It almost seemed as if there was a runner ahead of him. Most of the Europeans didn't even bother to be polite. They had heard of him and he was a bad risk. On the other hand he found the Chinese money-lenders too polite. They offered him tea and fluttered their hands expressively but couldn't see their way to lending him the money. He even tried one or two merchants who in the past had not been above buying the odd cargo of contraband goods, but in every case he was politely shown the door.

It was late in the afternoon when he turned into Charlie Beale's café. It was the one place where his credit was still good for a drink. He sagged down into a booth and, as he gratefully swallowed the cold beer the waiter brought him, someone sat down. Hagen looked across the table and saw Charlie Beale. Charlie smiled. 'Hello, boy! I hear you've made a proper cock-up of it this time and no mistake.'

Hagen gave him a tired grin. 'You mean the boat? I'll raise the money somehow.'

Charlie snapped his fingers and the waiter hurried over with a bottle of Scotch and two glasses. 'Have a decent drink, Mark,' Charlie said. He raised his glass. 'Luck, and you'll need it. The way I've heard it you'll be lucky if you can raise a brass farthing in this town. Somebody has put the word out. The shutters are up as far as you're concerned.'

Hagen was interested. There wasn't much

that went on in Macao that Charlie didn't know about. 'Who is it, Charlie?' he said. 'Is it Herrara the Customs chief? I know that bastard would love to see me lose the boat permanently.'

Charlie shook his head. 'It's a queer business,' he said. 'From what I can hear it's political. Are you in trouble with the Commies?'

Hagen didn't answer because suddenly a wild idea was smouldering in his brain. 'Charlie,' he said. 'How would you like to lend me ten thousand petakas?'

Charlie's eyes narrowed and his face became devoid of expression. He didn't laugh because he knew that Hagen must have some extraordinary proposition to make to him. 'You got something up your sleeve?' he said softly, and the Cockney accent of his youth became suddenly more pronounced.

'Something big, Charlie. Really big.'

Charlie stood up and motioned Hagen to follow him. He led the way upstairs and into his office. 'We can be private here,' he said. They sat facing each other across a wide desk. 'Let's hear it, boy, and it better be good.'

He was now the complete business man. Facts and figures were all that interested him. He listened to what Hagen had to say and then sat smoking a cigarette and thinking about it. After a while he opened a drawer and producing a map unrolled it on the desk. 'Look at this, boy,' he said. 'From here to the Kwai Marshes the coast is alive with gunboats and on top of them you've got the pirates. You wouldn't stand a chance.'

Hagen nodded. 'All right. It's going to be difficult, but it could be done.'

Charlie lit a cigarette thoughtfully and then said: 'Wouldn't you be better off in a motor sampan? You'd look like an ordinary fisherman from one of the coast villages.'

Hagen shook his head and said decisively: 'No, I don't agree. This whole thing has only one chance of success – speed. It's got to be done so fast that we're in and out with the gold before they know what's happened. To do that successfully I need a fast boat and mine's the best on the coast, as nobody knows better than you.'

Charlie Beale grinned. 'All right! So your

boat saved my neck once. I've paid for that favour a long time ago.'

Hagen nodded. 'I know, but I'm not asking for favours now. This is a business proposition.'

Charlie shook his head. 'Is it hell a business proposition. It's a gamble, but on the other hand I'm a gambler as well as being a business man.' He studied the map for a couple of minutes without saying anything and Hagen sat with sweating palms praying for the right reply. 'What would you need in the way of equipment?' he said at last.

Hagen had his answer off pat. 'Next to nothing. The boat is lying on a sandy bottom at a depth of twenty-five feet. The job should be easy. I've got an aqua-lung. A block and tackle to haul up the gold is easily rigged. The main thing is the money to pay that damned fine so I can get my boat back.'

Charlie nodded. 'That's not so bad. The whole thing could be done for peanuts.'

Hagen suddenly remembered something. 'One thing more,' he said. 'Important! I'll need some good automatic weapons and possibly a few grenades.' Charlie frowned and Hagen added, 'It would be silly to lose the gold simply because of an inability to defend the boat properly.'

'All right,' Charlie said. 'That would be difficult, though. It's pretty hard to get that kind of stuff these days. Who would you take with you?'

Hagen had the answer to that one, too. 'The girl, of course. She might get suspicious otherwise, and I need a deck-hand. O'Hara would be best. A Chinese boy might be a Commie plant.'

Charlie Beale snorted. 'What good would that old rummy O'Hara be? He gets the shakes if he doesn't have his two bottles of rot-gut a day.'

Hagen grinned. 'I know, but when he's sober he's a damned fine sailor and at least he can be depended on to keep his mouth shut.' Besides, he's a friend of mine.'

There was a long period of silence and a light breeze rattled the slats of the bamboo window-blind. Hagen lit a cigarette nervously and waited. Charlie studied the map and fiddled with an ivory-handled paper-knife.

Suddenly he straightened up and put down the knife. 'Okay, Mark,' he said. 'Come back tomorrow. Not too early, not too late. I'll think about it.'

Hagen kept his face straight as he left the office and clattered down the stairs and out into the crowded street. A tiny finger of excitement moved inside him and his face broke into a broad grin. Charlie had bitten. The whole thing was set. A feeling of tremendous confidence and hope surged through him. Very soon now, perhaps in a matter of days, he would be on that ferry going over to Kowloon. Then there would be a plane winging its way across the Pacific and then suddenly he knew that he didn't want to go back to the States. There was nothing left there for him. He considered the point and a smile tugged at the corners of his mouth. Ireland was the place. A country house with plenty of liquor and good horses.

It was thinking about Ireland that made him remember O'Hara and he decided to find the old man. He worked his way along the waterfront calling in all the bars and gin-palaces. He spent an hour in this way and was about to give up the search when he found O'Hara in one of the worst dives in Macao. A large French sailor with a Marseilles accent had the old man half over a table, holding him firmly with one ham-like fist while he poured beer over him with the other. Hagen pushed his way through the laughing, drunken crowd of spectators, picked up the nearest chair and crashed it down on the Frenchman's head and shoulders. The chair splintered a little and the man sagged to the floor without a sound. Hagen slung O'Hara over his shoulder and the crowd respectfully parted to let him through.

He called a rickshaw and dumped O'Hara in it, then walked beside it until they came to the seedy hovel the old man called home. He carried him upstairs and dumped him on the bed in his room. From the looks of him O'Hara had been on the bottle for at least two days. Hagen locked the door from the outside and put the key in his pocket.

Night was beginning to fall when he reached his hotel. There was a new desk-clerk on duty, a thin, vicious-looking Chinese. 'Any messages?' Hagen asked.

'No, Captain Hagen. No messages,' the man replied.

Hagen was half-way up the stairs when it suddenly occurred to him that the man had known his name and then he began to wonder what had happened to the other desk-clerk. He walked softly up to his door and stood listening for a while. He decided that he was being silly and unlocked the door and went in.

When he turned on the light there was a man sitting on the bed gazing pensively at the wall. He was small and dark and impeccably dressed in white sharkskin. His gloved hands were folded over a silver-topped Malacca cane. Hagen leaned against the door, lit a cigarette and waited. Small, black, shining eyes had swivelled to a position from which they could observe him. The man half-turned his body and, still remaining seated, raised his panama and said in clipped, precise English, 'Have I the honour of addressing Captain Hagen?'

Hagen decided that he was too charming.

The eyes were deadly and unwinking like those of a puff-adder, despite the polite, bird-like expression on the face. Hagen blew a cloud of smoke in his direction and said, 'Look, I'm busy, so kindly state your business and then get the hell out of here.'

The little man half-lifted his cane reprovingly and smiled like a father dealing with a recalci-trant son. 'Captain Hagen, how would you like to earn twenty thousand American dollars very easily? No risk, in fact no trouble at all.'

Hagen walked into the bathroom and came back with the gin bottle and two glasses. He poured the drinks and they sat side by side on the bed without speaking. He knew that this must be someone very special. A Russian working for the Reds in China would hold a very high position. They must be pretty determined to get their hands on that gold. He reached for the bottle and poured himself another drink. 'How are things in Moscow these days?' he said.

The Russian smiled and inclined his head. 'I bow to your perspicacity, Captain. However, I have not been in Moscow, or indeed in Russia, for ten years, and between ourselves' – and here he lowered his voice with a conspiratorial air – 'the arrangement suits me perfectly. I find the Oriental way of life very appealing, Captain. The standards, the moral values, even the food, are all infinitely more preferable. What comparison can be made between a brawny collective-farm girl and the fragile Eastern blossoms that are to be found in various parts of this city?'

The Russian's eyes became smoky and a dreamy look came over his face. Hagen shuddered with distaste but he had to find out what the other side were up to. He schooled his face to smile. 'How do I earn twenty thousand so easily?'

The Russian's face broke into a radiant smile and he stood up and formally clicked his heels. 'Ah, so we can do business? My name is Kossoff, Captain Hagen.' He extended his hand formally and then went on, 'My principals will pay you the agreed sum of money if you will lead them to the position of a certain boat which sank, I believe, somewhere in the vicinity of the Kwai Marshes.'

Hagen put back his head and laughed. 'What do you take me for?' he said.

Kossoff smiled thinly. 'I take you for many things, Captain, for you have been many things to many people. British naval lieutenant, American naval commander. How do you like your new role as protector of innocence?'

It was with difficulty that Hagen held himself in check. He said calmly: 'Your proposition stinks. Why should I tell you where the boat is for a paltry twenty thousand when I can get the gold myself?'

Kossoff squinted along his cane. 'Ah, but can you, Captain? I think not. In the first place you must raise the money necessary to retrieve your boat. Have you had any success, by the way? Secondly, you must leave Macao and enter the Kwai Marshes without being observed. An impossibility, my dear sir.' He smiled charmingly. 'However, as I cannot do business with you I must of necessity pay a call on Miss Graham. Women, I find, are so much more co-operative.'

Hagen was on him before he reached the

door. He grabbed him by the lapels and twisted the collar about his neck until the little black eyes protruded. 'You dirty little rat,' he cried. 'If you lay a finger on that kid I'll –' Instinct made him jerk his head to one side as he sensed a presence behind him. A leather, shot-filled sap grazed his shoulder and he jerked Kossoff round and into his assailant.

They must have been waiting on the balcony, he thought, as he turned to meet them. There were two of them, flat-faced Mongolians, not as big as Lee but large enough. He ducked under the arm of the nearest one, dug his right fist into the man's belly, and vaulted over the bed.

For a moment there was quiet, the lull before the storm. One of the men sat Kossoff in a chair and gave him a glass of water while the other faced Hagen across the bed, the leather sap twitching nervously in his hand. Finally Kossoff became articulate again. He fingered his throat gingerly with one hand and then pointed at Hagen and said softly in Cantonese: 'Beat him. Beat him but do not kill him.'

Hagen decided he had waited long enough. From the look of them Kossoff's apes would draw a very thin line between a beating and a killing. He gripped the edge of the blankets and, as he lifted them, sprang on to the bed. His hands spread and he threw the blankets as a fisherman casts his net, so that they enveloped Kossoff and the man who was standing beside him. Almost in the same motion he jumped feet foremost at the other man. The force of that terrific blow sent the Mongolian backwards, through the window and on to the balcony.

Hagen landed on his forearms in the classic Judo manner and twisted to face the other thug. In his effort to avoid the blankets the man had stepped back and fallen over Kossoff's chair bringing them both to the floor. As he cast the blankets aside and started to get up, Hagen kicked him in the face as he would have kicked a football, beautifully judged and timed.

Hagen stood breathing heavily as Kossoff scrambled to his feet and backed to the door. He pushed past the Russian, wrenched open the door and dragged the unconscious Mongolian outside. At the same moment the other man appeared from the balcony. He was doubled over in agony and there was blood oozing from his mouth. Hagen gestured fiercely and the man passed him and staggered along the corridor. They all went downstairs in procession, Hagen bringing up the rear dragging the unconscious man by the collar. The clerk pretended to be extremely busy as they crossed the hall.

On the other side of the narrow street there was parked a large American limousine that somehow looked familiar. The one who was still able to walk opened the door and Hagen bundled the other inside. As he straightened up he suddenly felt a slight prick as something needle-sharp nudged into his back. 'I underestimated you, Captain Hagen,' Kossoff said. 'A Judo expert. I must be more careful in the future. However, I win the trick, I think?'

'By one point,' Hagen said, bitterly.

The pressure was removed and he turned to find Kossoff replacing two feet of wicked-looking steel in the Malacca cane. Suddenly

Hagen felt utterly weary and deflated. The little street was empty and quiet. Through the darkness he could see traffic passing at the far end but somehow it seemed unreal and very far away. Even the sounds were subdued and meaningless. Kossoff said: 'You are surprised that I do not kill you? Allow me to explain. As I told you, I have not been to Moscow for ten years. The point is, Captain, that I do not intend to return to Russia at all if I can avoid it. I have what you would call a 'plum' job in China. I live very well indeed but my standard of living is threatened, Captain, and by you. The party is harsh with failures. If I do not get that gold I may very easily be recalled to explain my failure. However, I do not intend to fail.' He adjusted his tie and the angle of his panama. 'I give you two days in which to consider my proposition.'

Hagen decided that it would be pointless to tell him to go to hell. 'All right,' he said. 'I'll think about it.'

Kossoff got behind the wheel and said: 'My poor fellows. You were really extremely rough with them, Captain. Thank you for delivering them to the car. That's what I call service.'

'Go to hell,' Hagen told him. 'I only did it to keep the police out of this.'

'In two days, my friend.' The car slid away from the kerb and Hagen turned wearily and went back into the hotel.

He had a shower and changed and then came downstairs. He told the clerk to get someone to clean his room and that if anyone wanted him to say he had gone out for a drink. The clerk bobbed his head and Hagen went out of the front door. He stood outside for perhaps a full minute and then quickly went back into the hall. The clerk was speaking into the telephone. 'He has just left for the evening. I think –'

Hagen lifted the flap and stepped behind the desk. As the man backed away from him he grabbed him by the front of his jacket and pulled out the automatic with his free hand. He slammed the barrel twice against the man's face and the heavy metal opened a jagged groove down his right cheek. The man collapsed across the top of the desk, moaning bitterly, and Hagen said: 'I don't like snoopers. You'd better not be here when I get back.' He turned and left the hotel.

He walked to Clara Boydell's place, twisting and turning through back streets and stopping many times to see that he wasn't followed. When he reached the house it was a blaze of lights and there were many cars parked outside – some with diplomatic plates. He let himself in by the front door. The gaming tables that Clara ran on the ground floor were doing a roaring trade, and he could see her standing in the lounge talking animatedly to a group of distinguished-looking gentlemen. He went upstairs and asked a passing maid to show him to Rose's room.

The room was in darkness. A shaft of yellow light shone through the window from a lamp outside. The girl was lying under a mosquito net and he was unable to see her clearly, only to get a vague impression of rounded limbs and blue-black hair spread across the pillow. Faintly in the distance he heard a snatch of laughter and then the sad, sweet strains of a clarinet as the band started to play. Very quietly he tip-toed from the room.

He was tired when he reached his hotel. There was a smart-looking Chinese girl at the desk now. He asked her where the man was and she said that he'd left in a hurry. Her uncle, who was the proprietor, had been compelled to ask her to come at very short notice. It was really most inconvenient. Hagen agreed with her and went up to his room. Suddenly he was more tired than he had been in a long, long time. He flung himself down on the bed and lay staring at the ceiling and after a while it moved a little and then he was asleep.

He awakened suddenly and completely. Because he was not aware of the thing that had disturbed him, his hand slipped under the pillow and curled around the butt of the automatic. There was an urgent tapping on the door and the Chinese girl's voice said: 'Captain Hagen! Come quickly! There's an urgent telephone call.'

'Who is it?' he said through the door.

'No name. Lady say very urgent.'

He jerked open the door and rushed past her, taking the stairs three at a time. He stood at the desk and spoke into the receiver, 'Hagen here.'

'Mark, this is Clara. I'm sending Lee for you in a car. You'd better get here fast. They've kidnapped your girlfriend.'

Somehow her voice suddenly drifted away into the distance. For a moment he swayed as for the first time he realized that the girl was important to him, and then he recovered and said: 'Thanks, Clara. I'll be with you in fifteen minutes.'

He dropped the receiver and turned and ran past the astonished girl up the stairs to his room.

4

He had barely finished dressing when he heard the car brake to a halt outside. He ran downstairs, wrenched open the door, and scrambled into the rear seat. Before he could get the door closed the car had roared away from the kerb. They turned a corner on two wheels, scattering pedestrians, and then Lee turned into a maze of quiet back streets, driving like a demon.

Hagen had never felt so frustrated in his life as he did during the fifteen minutes it took them to reach Clara Boydell's place. He was desperately anxious to know what had happened and the only man who could tell him was unable to speak. He wondered what time it was and decided it must be about one in the morning. And then his waiting was over and the car turned in at the gates of Clara's house and skidded to a halt, scattering gravel.

The place was ablaze with lights and raucous with merriment as always. He ran up the steps and through the front door. A maid was waiting for him and pointed upstairs. He went up, two at a time, and suddenly Clara appeared at the top, a livid bruise on one of her cheeks. She was more angry than he had ever seen her. 'This way,' she grated and led the way down the corridor to the room Rose had been occupying.

The door of the room was standing open and the lock hung at a crazy angle. Hagen stepped into the room and glanced about him. As far as he could see everything appeared to be in reasonable order. There was only one thing missing – Rose. He slumped down on to the bed and fumbled in his pocket for a cigarette. He could only find an empty packet and he made quite an operation out of examining the packet and smoothing it between his fingers because a little voice inside was telling him to keep calm and to get a grip on his nerves. If he was to get the girl back it would need ice-cold thinking.

Clara offered him a cheroot and he lit it and inhaled the smoke gratefully. It seemed to put new life into him and he felt more calm. He squinted at Clara through the blue smoke. 'How did you get that bruise?'

She exploded. 'I got smacked down. Me, Clara Boydell, smacked in the puss by a little yellow bastard.' She went purple with rage at the memory.

'Simmer down,' Hagen said. 'If I ever run into him I'll give him your warmest regards. Now tell me exactly what happened.'

She shrugged. 'There isn't much to tell. About midnight a party of Chinese – four of them, I think – asked to see some girls. They were polite, well dressed. In fact they'd been at the tables for an hour and seemed well heeled. The maid took them up to the first floor and one of them gave her a clip on the jaw. They went along the corridor looking into every room and I can tell you it must have been embarrassing for some well-known citizens of this town. I was on the top floor entertaining the new Air Attaché from the French Embassy – quite a guy,' she added in a reminiscent mood.

'Get on with it, Clara,' Hagen said, impatiently.

'All right, lover. Anyway, I came down to find these guys dragging Rose along the corridor. I asked them what the hell they were doing and one of them smacked me on the jaw. They left by the back stairs. The gardener says there was a black limousine waiting at the rear.'

'Anything special about these characters?' Hagen said. 'Were any of them Mongolian by any chance?'

She shook her head. 'Definitely not, but I shan't forget the one who clipped me in a hurry. A nasty-looking little rat. Somebody had been carving his face up for him. One side was black and blue.'

Hagen felt a glow of satisfaction. At least he had a lead now. 'Good girl,' he said. 'I think I know who that punk is. Can I borrow Lee and your car for a couple of hours?'

She nodded. 'You can have anything you like just so you get that nice kid back in one piece.'

Hagen didn't waste time in further talk. Within seconds he was in the back of the car nursing the automatic as Lee threaded through the back streets. He slipped the automatic into his inside jacket-pocket and sank back in the upholstered seat. He knew that he had to move fast. Every second counted if he was to get Rose back unharmed. The car slowed to a halt and he wrenched open the door and darted into the hotel. The Chinese girl looked up from the book she was reading. Amazement showed on her face. 'Is everything all right, Captain?'

Hagen sagged on to the desk top. 'Anything but,' he said. 'I need some information badly. It's a matter of life and death. That lousy bastard who was working here before you, have you got his address?'

She bent down and searched under the desk for a moment and then she gave a little grunt of satisfaction. 'Sure. He ask for money to be sent to this address.'

Hagen grabbed the scrap of paper. 'Thanks, kid,' he said and ran out to the car again.

It took only five minutes in the car to reach the address. Hagen told Lee to stop at the end of the street. He didn't want to alarm their quarry before they got to him. They went the rest of the way on foot. The address was in a Chinese apartment house, reasonably clean and respectable. The apartment they wanted was on the ground floor and they moved up to the door silently and Lee bent down and listened at the keyhole. After a moment he straightened up and nodded and Hagen knocked softly on the door. Almost immediately there was a creaking of bed springs and a voice said in Cantonese, 'Who is there?'

Hagen answered gruffly, hoping the door would mask his foreign accent: 'Hurry up and open the door, fool. I have a message from the chief.'

There was a sound of cursing and the bed springs creaked again and after a few seconds the door opened a fraction. Hagen pushed on it sharply with all his weight and it burst open flinging the man back across the room and on to his bed. There was a stifled scream and Hagen saw a young, terrified Chinese girl, with bare shoulders, cowering back under the sheets. 'Keep your mouth shut if you know what's good for you,' he told her.

The door clicked into place behind him and he stood gazing into the hate-filled eyes of the erstwhile desk-clerk. He noted with satisfaction that one side of the man's face was terribly bruised and swollen. He turned and went to the window, and pulled down the blind. 'I'm not going to argue with you,' he said calmly. 'I want to know where they've taken the girl.' He turned to face the Chinese and the man spat in his face.

Hagen closed his eyes for a second. I mustn't kill him, he thought. He's got to talk. He must talk. He turned away, wiping the spittle from his face, and said, 'Lee, this is the man who hit Missee Clara.' Lee moved forward and something glowed deep in his eyes. 'Make him talk, Lee,' Hagen said. 'Do anything you have to, but make him talk.'

He turned his back and stood at the

window and peered through the slats of the blind out into the quiet street. He tried to ignore what was going on behind him but his mind refused to be baulked of its pleasure and he realized that his ears were cocked for each groan. Suddenly the girl said something in Cantonese so rapidly that he could not catch it and then the man said, 'No,' three times and each time he said it his voice was pitched a little higher. Suddenly he screamed and shouted in agony. Hagen turned quickly. Somewhere in the building he heard sounds of movement and he pulled Lee away and said to the man: 'Quickly now. Tell me where she is and I'll make him stop.'

Saliva dribbled from the corner of the man's mouth and tears oozed from his swollen eyes. Hagen shook him impatiently as the noises upstairs became more obvious and the man moaned through clenched teeth: 'The warehouse of Henry Wong on the waterfront. South side of the harbour.'

'And Kossoff – will Kossoff be there?'

'Yes, Kossoff will be there.' His head lolled to one side and he fainted.

At the same moment the girl began to scream loudly and piercingly and a thunderous knocking sounded on the door. Hagen ran to the window and jerked it open, grateful for the fact that the man lived on the ground floor. A moment later Lee was driving furiously through the back streets taking them away from the shouting and the hubbub behind them.

Hagen told him to take them to Clara's place. A vague idea was taking shape in his mind. He knew it would be useless to descend on the warehouse, gun in hand. Kossoff would simply blackmail him into submission by threatening to harm Rose. It would have to be something subtler than that. Whatever he did was going to be risky and he would have to move fast. Perhaps he was too late already. He shivered as he remembered the way Kossoff had talked about women.

As the car braked in front of Clara's door, Hagen leapt out and went straight through into her private lounge. She was waiting for him, puffing at a cheroot with ill-concealed anxiety. 'What happened?' she demanded. 'Have you found where she is?'

He nodded and picked up the telephone directory. A moment later he was dialling the number of Henry Wong's warehouse. Clara started to speak and he motioned her to silence as the receiver was lifted at the other end. There was silence and he listened to the sound of heavy breathing for a moment. He spoke quickly and economically: 'This is Hagen. Tell Kossoff I'm on the line. I think you'll find he'll speak to me.'

A voice said, 'Please wait,' and Hagen felt a little easier in his mind. So far so good.

The receiver was lifted and Kossoff spoke. Even over the wire he was unmistakable. 'Good morning, Captain. What a nice surprise.'

'Let's cut the pleasantries and get down to business,' Hagen said. 'You've fooled me. You've got the girl. I'm ready to do business with you now.'

'Ah, but do I need you now?' Kossoff said.

'Of course you do,' Hagen said. 'The girl is tough. She's had a rough time in Indo-China. She's just liable to die on you without opening her mouth.' There was a significant silence at the other end and Hagen continued: 'On the other hand she's in love with me. All I have to do is to come down there and tell her you'll kill me if she doesn't give you the information. She'll talk all right.'

There was still silence at the other end. Hagen could almost hear Kossoff's mind working. He was thinking that Hagen was a fool but that his plan had merit. After it had worked he could be conveniently killed. Kossoff spoke. 'I'll expect you within twenty minutes, Captain, and don't bother to bring a gun with you.'

The receiver clicked sharply into place. Hagen slammed a balled-up fist into his palm. 'It might work,' he said. 'It might just work.' He went over to Clara's desk and, opening a drawer, took out a .38 calibre pistol with a sawn-off barrel.

'What's going on?' Clara demanded. 'What the hell are you up to?'

'Get me some surgical tape,' he said. She went into the bathroom and came back with a roll and a pair of scissors. He took off his panama and placed the .38 inside, then he cut several strips of tape and stuck them criss-cross fashion so they held the gun in place. As he worked he told Clara what he intended to do.

'You're crazy. You'll never get away with it,' she said.

He adjusted the panama at the correct angle. There was no indication of the presence of the gun at all. 'What else can I do?' he said.

Clara's shoulders dropped suddenly and for the first time Hagen realized that she was an old woman. She opened a drawer in the desk and took out some banknotes. 'You'd better take them,' she said. 'You never know what may happen.' Tears began to spill from her eyes, coursing down her raddled cheeks, and Hagen patted her on the shoulder and then turned quickly and left the room.

There were still a few taxis waiting outside and he took the fastest-looking one and sank back in the seat and closed his eyes. It's got to work, he told himself. It must do. I've got to get her out of there and, suddenly, he realized that the first thought in his mind had been saving the girl for her own sake and not because of the gold. What's happening to me? he wondered, and the taxi stopped in front of a warehouse.

Hagen paid the man, who drove away. He turned and looked up at the decaying building. There was no mistaking the place. The name HENRY WONG – IMPORTER spread across the front of the building in peeling white paint. Somewhere out in the harbour a steamer's siren hooted mournfully and Hagen was afraid. As he moved towards the doors and knocked he was more afraid than he had ever been. A small service entrance was set in the framework of the great double doors through which the trucks passed. This was opened suddenly as if they had been watching him and a blinding light was directed into his face. 'Hands high and walk forward,' a voice said.

He did as he was told and then the main lights were turned on and he stood blinking, dark patches dancing before his eyes. Kossoff confronted him, a Lüger in his right hand.

He smiled. 'I hope for your own sake that you have obeyed my instructions, Captain.' He made a gesture and two men moved forward and ran their hands expertly over Hagen. They stood back, shaking their heads, and Kossoff smiled and put the Lüger in his pocket. 'Good, I am pleased with you, Captain. You show good sense. Follow me.' He turned and led the way across the vast, echoing floor.

As they mounted a flight of steel stairs Hagen glanced quickly behind him to size up the strength of the opposition. The other two men were typical toughs from one of the waterfront gangs. He felt less easy in his mind. He had been relying on having to deal with the usual fanatical amateurs but Kossoff had paid him the compliment of hiring professionals. Kossoff opened a door and they followed him in.

The room was a haze of tobacco smoke and brightly illuminated by a naked bulb that hung over a table in the centre of the floor. Four men were sitting round the table playing cards. Two of them looked Russian, another was Chinese and the fourth, who wore no jacket, could have been anything. They were a nasty-looking bunch. Kossoff stood watching them for a moment and as they continued to ignore him, lifted his foot under the table and sent it toppling to the floor. For a moment there was silence and then the one who was in his shirt sleeves spat out a curse in Portuguese. Kossoff slashed him across the face with his cane. 'It would be unwise for you to ever repeat such conduct, Cortez,' he said evenly. For a moment Cortez glared at him and then he smiled falsely and shuffled past Hagen to where his jacket was hanging on a hook.

Hagen was impressed. Kossoff had guts. He certainly didn't leave any doubt as to who was boss, even when dealing with rats. Hagen picked up a packet of cigarettes that had fallen to the floor from the table, and put one in his mouth. Kossoff smiled at him. 'Now then, Captain. Shall we join the lady?' He turned and said: 'Cortez and Li, come with us. The rest of you clear this mess up.' He unlocked a door with a key from his pocket and entered. Hagen followed him with Cortez and one of the Chinese gunmen bringing up the rear.

They walked into total darkness. There was a click as Kossoff switched on a light and they all stood blinking for a moment or so. The girl was on a rough camp-bed in the far corner. She sat up slowly, a dazed expression on her face. They had dressed her in the short trousers and smock of a Chinese girl and as she raised a hand to push back her hair one of the wide sleeves slid back, exposing vivid bruises on her arm.

Hagen stood facing her for a moment and then she recognized him. An expression of joy came into her eyes and she rushed across the room and flung herself into his arms. 'How very touching,' Kossoff said. 'I hate to interrupt so charming a reunion but, as they say, business before pleasure.'

Hagen gently disengaged himself from her arms and stepped back until he was standing behind her facing Kossoff. The Russian sat down and lit a cigarette which he placed in a long, amber holder. He blew a thin stream of smoke to the crumbling ceiling and said: 'Miss Graham, you don't seem surprised to find Captain Hagen here. Doesn't it seem a trifle peculiar?' She started to speak and he raised a hand. 'No, please don't interrupt me. Time is short and I will not bore you with the full details of how our mutual friend happens to be here. It is sufficient for you to know that if you persist in your refusal to give me the information I desire Captain Hagen will be the one to suffer.' He pointed at Cortez who was leaning against the door cleaning his nails with a spring-knife. 'Imagine what this gentleman would be able to do to the handsome captain with his little knife. Especially if we tied him to the bed.'

Rose raised a hand to her mouth and gave a terrified whimper. 'No, you wouldn't. You can't –'

Hagen decided it was time for action. He swung her round and slapped her back-handed across the face. 'Tell him what he wants to know, damn you!' he screamed as if panic-stricken.

He heard Kossoff's high, cackling laugh

and then a hand pulled him away from the girl and sent him reeling across the room. He allowed himself to fall across the bed as if off balance. Cortez moved towards him, the knife at the ready, an evil smile on his face. Hagen pulled off his hat and wrenched the gun free. He levelled it on a point just below Cortez's breast-pocket and squeezed the trigger twice. He was dead before he hit the floor.

As Hagen scrambled to his feet the Chinese dipped a hand into his pocket and pulled out an automatic. He was still trying to aim as Hagen shot him twice in the stomach. Kossoff already had the door open and the last two rounds chased him through, with no visible effect except to accelerate his progress. Hagen flung himself against the door, banged it shut, and rammed the bolt into position.

He picked up the automatic belonging to the second man who was coughing and writhing in agony on the floor. Hagen disregarded him and moved over to the window. It refused to budge when he tried to lift the sash and a quick examination showed that it had been screwed into place. He turned and gripped Rose by the shoulders. 'Are you all right? Did Kossoff harm you?'

She shook her head. 'He never laid a finger on me and the others couldn't get at me. They wanted to but they're all afraid of him. I think he was going to question me properly tonight.' She looked pale but managed to smile.

Hagen pushed her to one side and picking up a chair smashed it into the window. He battered away until the chair splintered into pieces but he had achieved his object and the entire window had dissolved into a snow-storm of flying glass. He leaned over the sill and looked down. Two storeys below was the wharfside. Only wings would help them there. He looked upwards and, as the sound of battering commenced on the door, he knew that their only chance lay on the roof.

The roof was flat but sloped slightly down to a gutter. It didn't look very safe but by jumping he decided he would be able to grip the guttering with his hands. He ducked back into the room and taking the automatic from his pocket gave it to Rose. 'There's a chance we might get on to the roof if the guttering holds. If it doesn't, I suggest you either blow your brains out or jump after me.'

She squeezed his hand once and then he was outside balanced precariously on the windowsill. For a moment he paused and then he jumped and gripped the edge of the gutter. It creaked ominously and sagged a little but didn't give way. He hung there for a moment and then heaved himself up until he could get his elbows above the edge. A moment later he was lying full length in the gutter, offering up a prayer to the carpenter responsible for the job.

He leaned over and extending his arm, shouted: 'Now, Rose! Now!'

There was a tremendous crash as the door burst open in the room and then a long, reverberating roll as she loosed off the entire magazine of the automatic. There was a confused shouting and screaming and a cry of agony and then she stepped lightly out on to the windowsill and reached up and caught hold of his hand. She was as light as a feather.

Before he realized it she was lying beside him in the gutter. She handed him the automatic. 'It was a good thing you gave it to me. I'm afraid I used all the rounds.'

He grinned. 'Good girl. I hope every one of them did its job well.' There was only the sound of men in pain from the room below. He scrambled on to the flat part of the roof and pulled her up beside him. 'The rest of them will be up here any minute,' he said. 'We've got to get moving.'

They began to run along the roof and had progressed only a few yards when there was a shout from the rear. Hagen turned and saw Kossoff and three men clambering out of a trap-door. He grabbed the girl's hand and they began to run. Occasionally they had to clamber over low roofs that divided one warehouse from another, for this part of the waterfront was lined with buildings. Finally they came to a low parapet and a narrow alley barred them from the next building. Hagen ran to the other side of the roof and looked straight down into the harbour. He recognized the place. They were on the roof of one of the granaries that loaded directly on to the ships. Behind them the hounds closed in. At that moment the moon came out from behind a cloud and glinted on the silver head of Kossoff's cane as he urged his men on. Hagen smiled at the girl. 'It's all of sixty feet down but the water is plenty deep enough. Are you game?'

'Have we any choice?' she said, simply.

Hagen stripped off his jacket and slipped the pistol into his trousers pocket. He gripped the girl's hand tightly and they clambered up on to the parapet. Behind him he heard Kossoff cry out and then they jumped.

The air rushed past his ears with a mighty roar and a thousand coloured lights seemed to dance through the sky like a stream of tracer bullets. He hit the water with a solid, forceful smack and seemed to go down and down into a black night that had no ending. A thousand years later he drifted lazily upwards out of the darkness and his head broke surface. He gazed up past the dark bulk of the warehouse at the stars and was aware of Rose floating beside him and realized that he was gripping her hand – had gripped it since the moment they jumped. 'Are you all right?' he said with difficulty, his lungs still gasping for air.

She nodded and gulped: 'I think so. But what now?'

He managed a grin. 'Can you swim a quarter of a mile?'

'I don't know,' was the reply.

'Well, now's the time to find out. We're going to swim across the harbour. That will put our friend up there off the scent. Just take it easy. A nice steady breast-stroke is the thing. If you get into difficulties don't worry, I'm here.'

They began to swim, steadily and slowly. The water was warm and the moon had gone behind a cloud again. There was only the two of them and the darkness. Kossoff and the gold and the whole world seemed to become unimportant and fade into the past. They swam side by side and occasionally their hands touched and Hagen felt curiously calm and at peace with himself.

They seemed to have been swimming for

an eternity when finally a mass of junks and sampans loomed out of the darkness and indicated that they had reached the North side of the harbour. They swam between the boats and landed at a flight of stone steps that led up to the wharf. They sat on the steps for a little while and Hagen asked her if she was all right. 'I'm fine,' she told him. 'Never felt better.' There was a distinct note of pride in her voice.

After a few minutes they climbed the steps and walked along the waterfront. There was an all-night bar nearby that Hagen knew of. When they entered it was empty except for a few drunks sleeping it off, sprawled across the tables. He put Rose in a booth and told the tired, disillusioned-looking bartender to take a couple of brandies to the table.

He went to the telephone and dialled Clara's number. The receiver was lifted sharply as if she had been waiting beside it. Hagen didn't explain anything. He simply gave her the address and asked her to send Lee down with the car to pick them up. He paid the bartender with a wet banknote and bought a packet of cigarettes. The man didn't quibble. His expression seemed to say that he'd got past being surprised at anything.

They sat smoking in the booth and Rose slumped wearily across the table and Hagen suddenly had a splitting headache and wanted nothing so much as a clean, cool bed for about fifteen hours. There was the sound of a car driving up outside and he gently shook Rose and they got up and went outside.

There was a blanket in the back of the car and as they drove away he wrapped it round her and slipped an arm about her shoulders. She snuggled close to him and just before she went to sleep, said softly, 'You're always there when I need you.'

Suddenly every muscle in his body seemed to give way. He sagged back in the seat, his mind in a turmoil, and wondered how on earth he was going to get out of this one.

5

Back at Clara Boydell's place two Chinese maids took charge of Rose and hustled her away upstairs to a hot bath. Hagen found Clara sitting at her desk with a large ledger open in front of her. She was wearing plain, horn-rimmed spectacles that gave her an oddly scholarly air. She ignored him for the moment and he helped himself to a brandy from the small bar that stood in the corner and drank it standing beside her, water dripping steadily on the thick carpet. She closed the ledger and removed the glasses. 'Queer time to be doing your accounts,' he told her.

She leaned back in her chair. 'I couldn't sleep until I knew what had happened.

Anyway, I wanted to see if I could catch that Indian accountant cheating me.'

'And have you?'

She shook her head. 'Not a chance. He's too smart, like some other people I know, but one day he's going to take just that one chance too many.'

Hagen smiled in acknowledgement of the hint and fished the .38 pistol from his pocket. 'Sorry it got wet,' he said.

She broke open the cylinder and six cartridge cases were ejected on to the desk. 'How many corpses did you leave lying around?'

He grinned. 'I wouldn't worry about that. The last thing these people want is the police butting in. The dead and dying will be in China proper by now, or I miss my guess.'

She lit a cheroot and gazed at him thoughtfully through the smoke. 'They didn't harm the kid did they?' He shook his head and she went on. 'Do you still intend to go ahead with this crazy scheme?'

'Why not? I'm beginning to feel lucky about the whole thing.'

'And you still intend to cheat the kid out of the gold?'

He put the brandy glass down carefully, anger stirring in him. 'Can you put me up for the night?' he said.

She nodded sadly. 'Sure – see one of the maids.' Suddenly she swore horribly and slammed a hand against the desk. 'Go on, get out of here, you bastard.' He closed the door softly behind him and went upstairs.

He had omitted to pull down the blind on going to bed so that warm sunlight falling across his face awakened him at nine-thirty. Surprisingly, he felt quite refreshed although he had slept for barely four hours. He stood under a hot shower for fifteen minutes and soaked the stiffness out of his muscles and then dressed in an immaculate satin gaberdine suit that some previous patron had carelessly left in the wardrobe after a visit. The suit was quite a good fit but the collar of the only reasonable shirt he could find was rather small. He omitted to fasten the top button and managed to hide the fact with an extra-large knot in the silk, hand-knitted tie that seemed to go with the suit.

He looked at himself in the mirror with a certain satisfaction and reflected that if he could lay his hands on that gold he could wear suits like this for the rest of his life. As he went downstairs he wondered if Rose would be impressed. He shook his head and decided that she was in his thoughts more often than she should be, crowding out important matters.

The house was quiet and still. He wasn't surprised, for, as a rule, even the staff seldom stirred before noon. He found some Chinese cleaning-women in the kitchen, who were extremely alarmed when he appeared, probably because they imagined he might report them to Clara for slacking. He soon established cordial relations after a few bawdy and bad jokes in Cantonese. Within a few minutes he was sitting down to a hastily improvised breakfast of grapefruit and an omelette.

There were several cars in the large garage at the rear of the building. He selected an old and rather battered station wagon, mainly because it looked inconspicuous, and drove down to the waterfront at a steady pace, trying to think of a plan of campaign for dealing with Charlie. He parked the station wagon in an alley at the side of the café and slipped in through a rear door.

The place was empty as far as customers were concerned and a large, lugubrious-looking negro was singing to himself as he swabbed the floor. When he saw Hagen he smiled, showing a row of perfect white teeth. 'Why, Mr Hagen, how's every little thing?'

Hagen grinned amiably. There was a bond between them of sorts, for the negro was an American. 'Hello there, Harry,' he said. 'Is Charlie about?'

Harry grinned. 'Now, Mr Hagen, you know he never shows his face before noon.'

Hagen nodded. 'I know, but I want to see him about something pretty important. I'll go on up.'

The negro shrugged and went back to his work and Hagen passed through a door at the rear of the café and mounted a flight of stairs. As he turned into a corridor that led into the private part of the building he saw a boy in a white drill jacket, carrying a covered tray. He stood at the door of Charlie's bedroom and the boy came towards him, a look of surprise on his face. Hagen looked at the tray. 'For Mr Beale?'

'Yes, sir. Mr Beale, he asked for breakfast in bed early this morning.'

Hagen took the tray from him. 'I'll take it in. Mr Beale and I have business to discuss.' The boy turned and walked daintily away down the corridor and Hagen knocked on the door and went in.

'Okay, son, put it by the bed.' Charlie had his head turned, as he arranged pillows into a back rest. When he saw Hagen he looked surprised and then grinned. 'Things must be in a bad way in the kitchen. When did the cook start you?'

Hagen poured coffee into a cup and handed it to him. 'Things aren't that bad yet.' He grinned and lit a cigarette. 'You know why I'm here, Charlie. What have you decided?'

Charlie handed him the coffee cup and started to cut into a hard-boiled egg. He took his time in replying. 'I've thought about it and the way I see it you don't stand a chance.'

Hagen's heart sank but Charlie went on. 'On the other hand I'm a gambler. The money it would cost is no more than my tables take in an hour. I always liked long odds.'

'You mean you'll do it?'

Charlie nodded. 'That's what I said.'

Hagen sat on the bed, and a feeling of elation surged through him. 'Thanks, Charlie,' he said. 'You don't know what this means to me.'

Charlie shook his head and lit a Turkish cigarette. 'Thanks, nothing. It's your neck. You've got a reputation for always having an ace up your sleeve. That's the thing that really influenced my decision.'

Hagen felt calmer. 'Okay, let's get down to business. This whole thing has to be played very cleverly and this is the way I want you to do it. You go to Herrara, the Customs chief, and tell him that I owe you a large sum of money. Tell him that I dropped it at your tables and can't pay. I'll give you a note showing that I've made the boat over to you. All you have to do then is discharge my debts and the boat is legally yours. If we do it that way Herrara will be happy because he'll think he's beached me and the story will get around the waterfront. If we're lucky it might put the Commies off the scent for a while.'

'Sounds good to me,' Charlie said. 'What do I do with the boat?'

'Have her taken to that beach-house of yours and we'll leave tomorrow night under cover of darkness.'

Charlie frowned and considered the plan. 'Don't you think you're rushing things a little?'

Hagen shook his head. 'On the contrary. I want to catch the opposition on the hop. With real luck I could be into the Kwai and out again before they've realized it.'

'Okay, boy,' Charlie said. 'Have it your own way. I'll have the boat and the necessary supplies taken out to my beach-house.'

'Don't forget the arms I asked for,' Hagen reminded him.

'They'll be there,' Charlie said. 'There's just one other thing. About the crew.'

Hagen was surprised. 'What about the crew? I told you O'Hara and the girl would be ample.'

Charlie shook his head and said softly: 'I like to lay off my bets as much as possible. Now what if you did manage to get the gold? You might get ideas.' He grinned amiably. 'Nothing personal, you understand, but we're all human.'

Hagen smiled slowly. 'All right. Point taken. What do you suggest?'

'I'm sending someone with you – just to protect my investment.'

Hagen laughed in amazement. 'Who have you got that's tired of life?'

Charlie lit another cigarette. 'The man I have in mind isn't tired of life exactly. Shall we say he's in no position to refuse. He's nowhere else to go – he depends on me.' He flung aside the blankets and got out of bed. 'This one's an American. A Navy man. Shot an M.P. in Tokio and had to leave in a hurry.'

Hagen shrugged. 'Okay, Charlie. If you want him to go, he goes. We need you to dispose of the gold, anyhow.'

He walked to the door and Charlie said, 'Give me a ring tonight and I'll let you know

if everything is going according to plan.'
Hagen nodded and left.

As he went downstairs he felt completely
sure of himself for the first time in years. He
was convinced that he had entered into one
of those lucky streaks when he could do
nothing wrong. He grinned at Harry and said:
'Set 'em up, boy. I'm celebrating a very satis-
factory piece of business.'

Harry went behind the bar and poured
whisky into two clean glasses. 'Here's luck,
Mr Hagen,' he said.

Hagen slid a note across the counter. 'Better
give me a bottle of rum, Harry. I'm going to
see O'Hara.'

Harry looked wise and passed a bottle of
cheap rum over the bar. 'I hear tell that man's
been on a three-day jag in every joint in town.
He's gonna wake up dead one mornin'.'

'Not that one, Harry. His stomach is lined
with teak.' He swung the bottle by the neck
as he walked out into the bright, hot street
that was already beginning to swelter under
the morning sun.

It was only when he reached the door of

O'Hara's room that he remembered that he
had taken the key away yesterday. He tried
to remember where he had put it and then
realized it had been in the pocket of the jacket
he had discarded on the warehouse roof.
He shrugged philosophically and, standing
back, lifted a foot and crashed it against the
lock. The door was worm-eaten and ancient
with the years. It splintered and rocketed
backwards.

He entered the dark room. The stench was
appalling and the air in the room was stifling.
He stumbled across to the window and
groped for the shutters. For several moments
he stood enjoying the cool breeze that was
sweeping in from the harbour and then he
turned to the bed and looked down at
O'Hara.

The old man lay on his back, mouth open
and twisted to one side. The soiled, filthy
sheets had draped on to the floor and he was
wearing only the singlet Hagen had left on
him when putting him to bed. Hagen threw
a sheet over the old man's nakedness and sat
down in the only chair the room could boast

and lit a cigarette. He gently fanned himself with his panama and looked at O'Hara with a mixture of disgust and pity. He had known him for a long time. The old man was a slave to rum. Some men had a woman, Hagen reflected. A beautiful, evil woman who could not be resisted. O'Hara just had the rum but the result was the same.

He wondered if he could ever sink to such a level and then his thoughts were interrupted by a long, shuddering sigh and O'Hara rolled over on to his back. Hagen leaned forward and saw that his eyes were open and regarding him with a peculiar fixed stare. The old man rubbed his knuckles into his bloodshot eyes and then heaved himself up until his back rested against the end of the bed. There was the same look of vague puzzlement and Hagen realized that O'Hara didn't recognize him.

A quiet space in time while a fly droned against the ceiling and the street sounds came faintly as from a great distance and then something clicked and a smile flickered around his mouth. 'Mark!' he croaked. Hagen unscrewed the cap of the rum bottle and filled a dirty glass that stood on the floor. The hand that reached for the glass trembled and the blue veins bulged through transparent, parchment skin. The glass tilted and a quarter of a pint gurgled down his throat. He reached for the bottle and Hagen passed it to him and watched him refill the glass and empty it again. He gave a long sigh of relief and lay back against the bed-head and, miraculously, ten years seemed to have dropped from his face. Hagen lit a cigarette and pushed it into the old man's mouth. For a moment they looked at each other and then an impudent grin appeared on O'Hara's face.

'You old bastard,' Hagen said in mock anger. 'You're incorrigible.'

'Well now, and why the harsh words, me darlin', and after you saving me from the "Gin-Trap" again?' He was referring to the special block in the city jail where they made alcoholics take the cure the hard way.

'You worthless old devil,' Hagen told him. 'If I didn't need you for a job I'd have left you to rot.'

The rheumy old eyes sparked. 'Is there much in it for me?' he said shrewdly.

Hagen walked over to the window. 'This could be a very tough one,' he said. 'Just about the toughest ever.'

'And how tough would that be?'

'I'd say about six to four against us getting out of Red China alive.'

The rum gurgled. 'Is that all? Sure now, at my age I'm past caring very much one way or the other. I wouldn't be missed and that's a fact.'

Hagen swung round. 'Listen to me, you old reprobate. If you can stay sober for a couple of days we won't die. You'll have enough money to go back to Kilkenny or Downpatrick or wherever the hell you started out from. You'll be able to die in bed like a gentleman.'

O'Hara's eyes blazed with excitement. 'You wouldn't kid me would you, lad?' He gazed at Hagen in awe and the empty glass slipped from his nerveless hand. 'You wouldn't kid an old man?'

Hagen threw a couple of banknotes on the

bed. 'Get yourself cleaned up. Have a steam-bath or something. Taper off on the liquor and get to bed early tonight. Tomorrow morning I want you to go to Charlie Beale's beach-house. You'll find the boat moored there. Check the engines.'

'You can rely on me, lad.' His voice trembled with excitement.

As Hagen opened the door a thought struck him. 'Whatever you do keep your mouth shut. Understand?' The old man winked and placed a finger against his nose and Hagen grinned as he closed the shattered door.

His next call was at his hotel. There was no one behind the desk and he went up to his room and started to pack his things. His worldly goods fitted into one suitcase and an old naval duffel-bag and there was room to spare. When he came downstairs again the proprietor was behind the desk. His fat and oily face beamed with pleasure and changed abruptly when Hagen asked for the bill. Hagen ignored him and pushed the money across the counter. The man pursued him to the door wringing his hands. 'But what is wrong, Captain? Are you not satisfied? Is the service not to your liking?'

Hagen grimaced. 'Service? What service?'

The man pawed at his sleeve. 'Perhaps my niece has not been accommodating? I could have a word with her.'

Hagen dropped his luggage and swung the man round. He booted him in the rear with all his force and had the satisfaction of seeing him stagger across the hall and fall over a chair. He picked up his bags again and left the place for the last time.

As he drove back to Clara's he was still thinking about the incident and he suddenly saw it in a symbolic light. He hadn't just left that particular hotel for good. He had left behind all the waterfront dives and flea-pits. In a way the hotel had represented the life he had been living for so long. By leaving the hotel he was also discarding a way of life. Once he could get his hands on that gold . . . and then he suddenly knew that even if he failed he wouldn't have to return to the old life because he would be dead.

The idea seeped into his mind and a wave

of coldness ran through him so that he shivered. As he turned the station wagon into the garage he vowed that nothing was going to stand in his way – not any person or any thing.

The house was still quiet. He went up to his room and dumped the luggage and then he tip-toed into the girl's room to see if she was awake. She was sleeping quietly, her head pillowed on one arm. He closed the door softly and went back to his own room. Suddenly he felt inexpressibly weary. He peeled off his jacket and flung himself down on the bed and in a moment was asleep.

When he awakened it was evening and shadows darkened the corners of the room. She was sitting on the edge of the bed looking at him and as his eyes opened a smile came to her face, warm and wonderful, as though a lamp had been turned on inside her. 'Hello!' he said. 'How do you feel?'

She pushed a tendril of dark hair back. 'Fine! Just fine. It all seems like a bad dream.'

He yawned and ran his fingers through his hair. 'Hell, I feel foul. My mouth tastes of mud.'

'I came to warn you,' she said. 'Dinner is at six and Clara says no excuses accepted. You've got about twenty minutes.'

He got off the bed and opened the suitcase and took out his razor. 'I'm going to have a quick shower and shave,' he told her. 'Shan't be long.'

The stinging lances of water invigorated him and by the time he had dressed again his body was glowing and alive. When he came back into the room she was sitting on the edge of the bed examining a photo in a leather case. He cursed softly at his clumsiness in leaving the suitcase open. She looked up and smiled apologetically. 'I'm sorry. I saw it on top of the other things. I couldn't resist peeking.'

Hagen shrugged. 'It doesn't matter.' He hadn't looked at the photo in a long time. The man on it was a stranger. A good-looking, clean-cut young naval officer who had died a long time ago.

'You looked different then,' she said. 'About the eyes and the mouth. Now you seem bitter.'

He nodded. 'Only a little, though. It's something life does to you.' He looked again at the photo as he adjusted his tie. 'Ah, halcyon days.'

She said, very quietly, 'What happened?'

For a second he was tempted to cut her off sharply, to tell her, to mind her own business, and then he suddenly realized that he wanted her to know and to understand. He walked over to the window and stood looking out, trying to get it clear in his own mind. 'It was one of those things. You never know when they start. Perhaps the day you're born – I don't know. When I finished college my father sent me to finish my education in Europe. I was at Oxford when the war broke out in 1939. I joined the British Navy. My old man was hopping mad. After Pearl Harbor I transferred into the American Navy. Finished the war as a lieutenant-commander. The trouble was that I liked the Navy but my father couldn't see it. Wanted me to be a stockbroker in the family firm. I refused, so he cut the cash.'

'Was that important?' Rose said.

117

He turned and smiled at her. 'I'm afraid it was. I had expensive tastes, particularly in women. The pay didn't stretch far enough. I was in charge of a messing account. I borrowed some cash against my next pay cheque and unfortunately the auditors arrived.' He laughed harshly. 'You know, it's damned funny, but in cases like mine the auditors always seem to come early.' He lit a cigarette, suddenly tired of the story, and added: 'I was asked to resign. Of course everyone got to know. The Navy is just one big, happy family. My old man gave me a thousand dollars and told me to vanish.'

'And so you came to Macao?'

He nodded. 'By way of Africa, India and various other places. I've been here about four years now.' He looked moodily out of the window. 'It's bloody funny how one little mistake can mean so much.' Abruptly he swung round and laughed brightly. 'But that was in another country, as the playwright said.' He picked up his jacket. 'Come on. Let's get something to eat.' He held open the door for her. For a moment she stood gazing steadily at him and then she walked out, an expression of puzzlement on her face.

Dinner wasn't a success. Clara had little to say and Rose Graham sat wrapped in her own thoughts. Hagen wished he hadn't told her about himself. It was as if she had built up a picture of him in her mind and he had spoiled it for her.

After dinner he slipped into Clara's office and telephoned Charlie Beale. When he replaced the receiver after a short conversation he was satisfied. Everything had apparently gone without a hitch and the boat was already on its way to the private inlet near Charlie's beach-house. As he turned to leave the room Clara entered. 'Just using your phone,' he said.

'Are you still going through with it?'

He nodded. 'Yes, everything's fixed. I've got the boat back, supplies, everything I need.'

'What about the kid?'

He suddenly felt really angry. 'For God's sake, Clara, why must you keep harping on that? I've told you she'll be well taken care of. Isn't that enough?'

'Is it?' she said. 'Do you really think that yourself?'

He pushed past her and wrenched open the door. 'I don't want to discuss it any more. And don't worry – we'll be off your hands soon enough. We're leaving in the morning.'

He went up to his room and lay on the bed in the dark, smoking furiously and hating Clara and the world, but, most of all, hating himself. There was a click and then a shaft of light moved across the floor as the door opened. He lay there waiting as she crossed to the bed and then he could smell the fragrance of her hair and she sat down on the edge of the bed and took his hand. 'Are you all right?' she said.

He allowed his hand to remain in hers. 'Yes,' he said. 'I'm fine.'

There was a small silence and she said: 'What happened today? Did you have any luck?'

He told her about Charlie Beale, omitting the fact that Charlie wanted a cut of the gold for his help. 'Charlie owes me a few favours,' he told her. 'Naturally he'll have to be reimbursed out of the proceeds of the gold, and the two men I'm taking as deck-hands – they'll have to be well paid.'

She accepted his explanations without argument. 'And you,' she said. 'What payment will you expect?'

For a moment time stood still as they both waited there in the darkness and then Hagen pulled his hand gently from her grasp and said: 'Better go to bed. Get all the sleep you can. You'll be needing it, believe me.'

He knew that she stood up and then he was aware of her walking away towards the door. She paused and her voice said softly: 'I want you to know that I understand. Truly I do.' The door opened briefly and closed again.

He lay in the darkness and after a while he stubbed out his cigarette and then there was no light at all and the nothingness pressed in on him and suddenly coldness spread through his body and he was afraid. He turned and buried his head in the pillow.

6

They left shortly before noon on the following day. The problem of getting to the beach-house unobserved was solved when Hagen noticed a laundry van parked outside the kitchen. A quiet chat with the driver and a liberal tip ensured that, when the van left, Hagen and the girl were safely hidden in the back amongst the bundles of dirty washing.

At the last moment they had missed Clara and she was nowhere to be found. Hagen wasn't surprised. She had treated him pretty coldly and for a while he had wondered whether she might tell Rose the truth about the whole scheme. He heaved a sigh of relief as the van jolted out of the side entrance and turned into the road. 'Well, we're really on the way now,' he said.

Rose nodded. 'Do you think all this secrecy is necessary?'

He considered the point for a moment before replying. 'Yes, it's worth it if only because it will keep Kossoff guessing. I don't think he's in Macao. I wouldn't be surprised if he's in China. Remember, he knows that whatever happens we've got to arrive at the Kwai Marshes at some time or other.'

'Then what chance have we got?' Rose said.

He laughed grimly. 'We've got one chance,' he said, 'and that's to get into those marshes and out again before he realizes it. That's why I want to leave tonight if we can possibly manage it.' He lit a cigarette and added: 'It all depends on what shape the boat's in. I hope that swine Herrara hasn't knocked her about at all.'

'You love that boat, don't you?' she said. 'You spoke about her then as if she was a woman.'

He grinned. 'Yes, I do think quite a lot about *Hurrier*.'

'*Hurrier*,' she said. 'What a peculiar name. What made you choose it?'

'Because that's exactly what she is. She belonged to a dope smuggler who was shot dead in a fight with the Customs near Java. I happened to be in Sourabaya when she was auctioned off. I had a pocketful of money and bought her. She's forty-five feet long, diesel engines. Ex-Japanese Navy, though what they used her for is anybody's guess.' He smiled to himself. 'Just about the fastest thing in these waters.'

Rose chuckled softly. 'I wonder if you'll ever think as much about a woman as you do about that boat,' she said, and then suddenly coloured and lapsed into silence.

The van jolted to a standstill and they opened the doors and scrambled out. They were standing in a small enclosed courtyard. Hagen paid off the driver and said to Rose, 'How do you like it?'

She looked at the gardens which could be seen through an archway in the wall, and at the rear of the cool, pleasant-looking house. 'It's nice.'

'You haven't seen anything yet,' he said. At that moment two Chinese house-boys emerged from the rear door and fought for possession of their luggage. Finally they had things sorted out to their satisfaction and led the way into the house and along a narrow, dark passage, which led into a spacious suntrap of a lounge.

The lounge jutted out from the rest of the house and the three outside walls were almost entirely constructed of glass. The view was breath-taking and Rose stood in the middle of the floor and clapped her hands like a small child. 'Oh, Mark,' she sighed. 'It's wonderful.' She opened one of the french windows and ran out on to the terrace.

Hagen told one of the house-boys that they were going down to the boat and to ask Charlie to join them when he arrived, then he followed Rose out on to the balcony. He leaned on the balustrade beside her so that their shoulders touched, and looked out over the blue-green China Sea. Beneath the terrace, the cliffs dropped a good hundred feet down into a small, funnel-shaped inlet. From that height they were able to see quite clearly the different shades of green in the waters of the inlet caused by the coral ledges at varying depths. The boat floated motionless beside a stone jetty that pushed out from the bone-white sand. There was no sign of life. Hagen said: 'O'Hara should be on board. Let's go down and have a look.'

The beach was reached by a series of stone steps that zigzagged in a haphazard, lazy sort of way across the face of the cliff. Hagen was sweating when they reached the bottom. They walked along the jetty, the heat from the stones striking up through the soles of their shoes, and as they neared the boat they could hear a muffled banging. 'These stones are almost red-hot,' Rose said.

He nodded. 'Yes, and be careful not to touch any metal when you get on the boat. You'll probably burn yourself.'

They dropped down on to the deck and Hagen led the way into the wheelhouse. Everything seemed in perfect order and he ran his fingers over the brass-mounted compass with deep and conscious pleasure. The windows were grimy and smeared and, as he picked up a rag and wiped them, Rose chuckled deep down in her throat. He suddenly felt awkward and she smiled and touched his arm impulsively. 'I'm sorry. I wasn't making fun. It's just that you make it so obvious how much you think of this boat.'

He grinned. 'I know, I'm like a fussy old woman.' He led the way out on to the deck again and said, 'You'd better meet O'Hara.'

She followed him down the short steel ladder that led into the cramped, stifling engine-room. It was so hot that sweat suddenly poured from his face in tiny rivulets and he turned to her and pointed upwards. Rose, who was already looking faint, clambered back on deck.

The noise was deafening and he could see O'Hara in a corner banging a cylinder casing back into position with a heavy hammer. Hagen touched him on the shoulder and O'Hara turned and smiled and stopped banging. The reverberations died away. 'So you got here at last.' He was wearing only a greasy pair of shorts and a sweat rag.

'What shape is she in?' Hagen asked.

'Perfect, lad. Just a few odd jobs and she'll be ready for anything. The tanks are brim-full. Charlie saw to that.'

Hagen patted him on the shoulder. 'Good man! I knew I could depend on you. Now come on deck and meet the girl.'

They found Rose sitting on a coil of rope fanning herself with Hagen's panama. He introduced her to O'Hara and the old man's eyes gleamed approval. 'It's the first time I've known this one here to show any taste at all,' he told Rose and she glanced at Hagen and smiled.

They sat down on the deck, their backs resting against the bulkhead, and Rose and Hagen smoked cigarettes and O'Hara his foul old pipe. They didn't talk about the trip or the sea. In fact, their conversation seemed to touch on nothing connected with the Orient at all. O'Hara reminisced about his boyhood in Ireland, about the fishing and of going out with a gun in the early morning, and Hagen found himself remembering his early years in Maine and Connecticut. Summers sailing with the fishermen off Cape Cod and the excitement of returning home to a New England white Christmas. It was a lazy, happy sort of conversation of the kind one only has in the company of good friends. The talk ebbed and flowed like the tide and occasionally there were short periods of silence and these periods were more marked because of the stillness of the hot afternoon when the sea was like a mirror – still and resting in the heat.

It was during such a period of silence that it occurred to Hagen that he had not fully explained the situation to O'Hara. It was only by good fortune that the journey ahead of them and the eventual disposal of the gold had not been mentioned. He stretched himself lazily and said, 'I think we'd better have a look at that cylinder casing.'

O'Hara looked at him in surprise and then he nodded. 'All right, lad.'

Hagen told the girl to stay on deck and she nodded sleepily and stretched out in the slight shadow of the bulwark and he and

O'Hara went below. Going into the engine-room was like diving into a pool of water. The heat was so tremendous that he had to make a distinct physical effort to force a passage through. He stripped off his shirt and squeezed into the narrow space beside the engine and began to screw the casing into place. O'Hara held it steady for him and as they worked Hagen explained the situation. When they had finished they backed out to the foot of the ladder and stood there for a moment trying to catch a breath of compar-atively cool air. 'There is an unpleasantness to the whole affair,' the old man said slowly.

A sudden flash of irritation surged inside Hagen. Was everyone against him? 'Don't be a bloody fool,' he said. 'The girl won't suffer, I promise you. She'll get a full and equal share. Enough to keep her in luxury for years. When the time comes I'll explain things to her. She'll come round to my way of thinking.'

O'Hara sighed. 'Aye, we'll have to hope that she will. But I can't say I like it at all.'

They mounted the ladder to the deck and as they went towards Rose she made an exclamation of disgust. 'Look at your trousers,' she said to Hagen. He glanced down and saw a large smear of grease where he had been kneeling. 'Why can't you put on some working clothes?'

He grinned amiably and retreated to the main cabin. He changed quickly into a pair of faded blue denims, sweat shirt and rope-soled shoes. The outfit was completed by a battered and salt-stained cap, a relic of his Navy days. When he came out on deck again she clapped her hands and said approvingly: 'That's much better. You look like something out of a Hemingway novel.'

He didn't find time to reply because, with a great roaring that fractured the afternoon stillness in a thousand places, a small motor boat swept into the inlet through the narrow passage that led from the sea. The motors cut suddenly and the boat drifted against the jetty with a gentle bump. Charlie Beale came towards them, a genial smile on his face. 'Hello there!' he called.

Hagen was watching the man who was busy securing the motor boat to the jetty.

How can one explain the inexplicable? He wondered. He had liked Rose from the moment he had seen her without knowing anything about her. In that same positive way he disliked the man who followed Charlie along the jetty and jumped down on to the deck of *Hurrier*. 'Meet Steve Mason, the other member of your crew,' Charlie said, waving a hand. Hagen shook hands briefly and Mason looked at him quizzically, a peculiarly mocking expression in his blue eyes. He was a large man, heavily built, with sun-bleached, fair hair and a red, slightly freckled face.

As Hagen assessed the man, introductions took place automatically all round. Charlie was very impressed with Rose and she seemed to take to him at once. They led the way back up the steps towards the house and Hagen and Mason followed. Half-way up the cliff Mason offered him a cigarette and they stopped to light up. As he flicked the match away Mason said, 'You don't remember me, do you?'

Hagen looked at him in puzzlement and then suddenly something rose to the surface of his consciousness. 'I knew you in the Navy, didn't I?'

Mason nodded. 'Correct! Only a short time – two weeks to be precise. I was an ensign on the *Johnson* and you were "Exec.". I didn't like you at all, Hagen. The white-haired boy with the medals and all the combat experience with the British. I was Gunnery Officer and during our trials at Pearl you were never off my neck. You told the old man I was incompetent and had me transferred to H.Q. I finished the war in a desk job.'

Hagen forced a smile and began to climb the steps again. 'Then I did you a good turn,' he said. 'You know what happened to the *Johnson*. There were only eighteen survivors.'

'I notice you managed to be one of them,' Mason said with a sneer.

Hagen tried to keep the conversation on an even keel. 'What made you shoot that M.P. in Tokio?' he said.

Mason laughed bitterly. 'What a bloody mess that was. I had a damn good job when Korea started and they called me back. I was a lieutenant-commander in charge of a supply depot in Japan. I was doing all right for myself on the side, working the black-market and giving contracts to the right people. Unfortunately some nosy bastard found out about my three bank accounts.' He laughed harshly. 'I didn't want to shoot that guy but if I hadn't done I'd have been in a cell now. It was him or me.' In some strange way there was real regret in his voice.

'Charlie explained about this job, didn't he?' Hagen said.

'You mean about the girl not knowing what's going to happen to the gold? Oh, sure. It's a neat scheme. Congratulations.'

There was again a sneer in his voice and Hagen restrained himself forcibly and ground his nails into the palms of his hands. 'Just remember one thing, Mason. You're simply a hired hand on this trip. You do what I say and when I say. Understand?'

Mason's hand swung up in a mocking salute. 'Aye aye, Captain.' He grinned wickedly and added: 'That's a nice girl. It should prove an interesting trip.'

Hagen turned and gripped him by the

lapels and pushed him back until they teetered on the brink of the path. 'There's a hundred feet of eternity behind you, Mason, and I wouldn't need much persuasion to push you into it. Keep your lip buttoned and your hands off the kid. Understand?'

Something flickered in Mason's eyes and then a smile came to his lips. 'Sure! I get you. Don't get yourself worked up.'

Hagen was trembling when they came out on to the cliff top. As they paused for breath Rose shouted from the terrace: 'Hurry up you two. Lunch is ready.'

Hagen started forward and Mason gripped him by the arm and swung him round. 'Just one thing, pal. I'd be obliged if you'd keep your hands off me in future.' For a moment they stood, toe to toe, and then Hagen smiled slowly and turned away.

The lunch was pleasant enough though spoiled for Hagen by the company. Mason deliberately cultivated Rose and by the end of the meal she was calling him Steve. After lunch Charlie had drinks served on the terrace and Hagen helped himself liberally to the gin and sat scowling at Mason and Rose who occupied a double swing-chair together. He felt irritated and annoyed and for some indefinable reason he longed to rush over and smash his fist into Mason's face. Charlie was joining in with them and must have related some funny story because suddenly they all burst into roars of laughter. Hagen's grip tightened on the stem of his glass and he said roughly, 'Don't you think we ought to go over the situation, Charlie, now that everyone is present?'

They went into the sun lounge and Charlie produced a map and Hagen indicated the route and explained the difficulties and dangers. He told them that he calculated the trip would take twenty-four to twenty-six hours. Charlie began to work out figures on a sheet of paper. After a while he gave a satisfied grunt and said: 'I reckon you should be there sometime tomorrow night. If Miss Graham can find the spot where the launch sank without any trouble you should be in the right lagoon on Friday. You might even be able to start diving on that day. Whatever happens you should be ready to leave during darkness on Saturday night.'

'But that will mean a run back to Macao in daylight,' Hagen said. 'We'd never get through the Straits of Hainan.'

Charlie grinned knowingly. 'This is where the clever bit comes in. I have a ship which is passing through that region from Haiphong to Macao. I've instructed the captain to rendezvous a mile off-shore on Sunday morning. He should be there about six. He'll give you a couple of hours to get out of those marshes. If you don't make it by eight o'clock then you won't be coming and he'll leave.'

There was a pregnant silence and Mason said, 'Thanks for being so cheerful.'

Charlie led the way into the next room and made a sweeping gesture with one hand. Spread out on the floor on a groundsheet were two Thompson sub-machine-guns, a couple of Garrand automatic rifles and a box of grenades. There were several clips of ammunition and all the stuff looked new and unused. 'Are we starting a war?' Mason said.

Hagen nodded with satisfaction. 'Just one

more thing, Charlie,' he said. 'Dynamite. I might have to do some blasting.'

Charlie grinned. 'I figured on that,' he said, 'and I've got you something better.' He opened a drawer and took out a belt with several pouches in it. 'This stuff was used by Commandos in the war. It's plastic, waterproof, and can't go off unless it's detonated.'

'That's the stuff for me,' Hagen said. Mason had picked up one of the Garrands and was explaining how it worked to Rose. For a moment Hagen watched them moodily and then he turned to O'Hara and said: 'Come on! There's plenty for you and me to do on the boat.'

He imagined, as he went out on to the terrace, that she had called his name, but in his sudden blind, unreasoning anger he strode furiously to the cliff edge and began to descend the path. O'Hara hurried protestingly after him, cursing all the way. When they reached the beach he said, 'What's got into you, lad?'

Hagen shook his head. 'I don't know. I really don't know. Maybe I'm just scared now that we're actually going. Forget it and let's get things ship-shape round here.'

They slaved until five o'clock in the engine-room, stripped to the waist, sweat pouring from them. The house-boys came down carrying the guns and equipment, making several trips. There was no sign of Rose or Mason and, as he toiled in the heat, Hagen imagined them sitting in the air-conditioned lounge, sipping cool drinks and talking – perhaps even making love. He swore violently and went up on deck. He stood at the rail breathing deeply, looking down at the green water, and then she called his name and he turned to see her struggling along the jetty, preceded by the two house-boys carrying several boxes.

She looked cool and crisp in her linen suit and Hagen turned quickly to go below. 'Mark!' she called. 'Hang on a minute. I haven't had a chance to talk to you since lunch.' She stood on the jetty and looked down at him. 'What have you been doing?'

He spread his hands and said sarcastically: 'Oh, a few unimportant little jobs. I hope you and Mason have been enjoying yourselves.'

A shadow crossed her face and she said to the two house-boys, 'Take the boxes through into the galley.' She turned again to Hagen. 'That's the food. I've been preparing it. Mr Beale and Steve went into Macao. They'll be back at seven.'

He was thunderstruck and filled with self-loathing and yet, in his childish desire to hurt her, said: 'Well, you seem to prefer his company to mine. That's pretty evident.' He turned and dived over the rail into the water.

He swam down to the sandy bottom, which at that point was about three fathoms deep, and the water was of a coolness he had forgotten existed. As he floated upwards all the heat and the itch and the sweat were washed away and he suddenly knew what a fool he was. He broke surface and floated for a moment, wondering what he could say, and then he saw her, running along the sands on the far side of the inlet. He began to swim with a fast crawl-stroke that carried him across the narrow waters of the inlet in a few seconds. She dodged into the rocks that lined the long passage that led out to the sea but her skirt hampered her and she fell in the soft sand. She scrambled to her feet and continued to run. Hagen swam through the passage and when she came out of the rocks and faced the sea he was standing, ankle deep in the soft sand, waiting for her.

She was crying bitterly. She backed away from him into a little sand-filled hollow surrounded by rocks, tears coursing down her cheeks. He moved forward and gripped her by the shoulders. 'I'm sorry,' he said. 'I didn't mean it. It's the heat. It's enough to drive a man mad.'

'Oh, Mark,' she cried brokenly. 'I love you so much.'

For a moment his grip relaxed and then his arms enfolded her, crushing her against his chest. Water dripped from his face, and he said, 'This isn't going to do your suit much good, is it?'

Her hands pulled his head down and her mouth sought his and then he lifted her and gently laid her down in the soft sand. For a while he held her close while her body trembled and then she began to strain against him convulsively and her arms tightened about

142

his neck. For a moment his mind struggled against what was happening and then his control snapped. It was as though a great wind gathered them up and swept them away on a journey to the other end of time.

When they returned to the boat they walked hand in hand like children. O'Hara was lolling on deck smoking his pipe. The linen suit was badly crumpled and stained with salt water but there was no way they could hide it. O'Hara tried to look unconcerned and said: 'Charlie was looking for you. He wants you up above for dinner at eight.'

'Thanks,' Hagen said. 'We'll be there.'

The old man made a great play of taking out a silver pocket-watch and looking at it. 'Well, now,' he said. 'If I were you, I'd hurry. It's half past seven now.' Rose gave a startled yelp and fled below. The old man winked solemnly at Hagen. 'Amazing how time passes in certain situations,' he observed. Hagen pushed his cap down over his eyes and went below to change.

The dinner was superb. Charlie had obviously decided to make it something of an occasion. Hagen felt warmly content and as he watched Rose chatting animatedly to Mason he no longer felt jealous. She was bound to him now. He knew that with a sureness that was absolute. Once or twice she turned and looked at him and wrinkled her nose and a tiny smile played around the corners of her mouth.

Afterwards they gathered for drinks on the terrace and sat in the dusk chatting quietly. Hagen felt calm and warm inside. It was one of those moments of peace that sometimes come before periods of stress and danger. He had experienced them during the war and now, as then, was grateful.

Charlie and the two house-boys came down to the jetty to see them off. It was a warm, soft night with a luminosity shining from the sea. There was no moon for heavy cloud banked low over the horizon as though a storm were in the offing. Hagen pressed the starter and the engine roared and spluttered into life as if angry at being awakened from a sound sleep. The house-boys cast off for them and O'Hara and Mason hauled in the lines. The boat drifted away from the jetty and poised, almost motionless, for a moment. 'Good luck!' Charlie's last hail sounded detached and unreal and far away.

Hagen was aware of Rose standing at his shoulder. He grinned. 'Well, angel. Here we go.' She smiled back at him, confidently and in complete trust. He opened the throttle and as *Hurrier* strained forward with a sudden surge of power, he took her through the passage out into the China Sea.

7

Rose went below and after a while Hagen called Mason into the wheelhouse and told him to take over. He spent a thoughtful twenty minutes with charts and navigational instruments and then gave Mason a course. 'I'll get O'Hara to relieve you in a couple of hours,' he told him and went below.

He rummaged about in his duffel-bag until he found the Colt automatic which he had cleaned and oiled and replaced in the polished leather holster that still bore the legend USN. He strapped the holster to his waist and went into the galley and found Rose making coffee. There was a smudge of soot on her face. He laughed and said, 'So you cook as well.'

She grimaced. 'I'll have you know this cooker blew back in my face twice before I managed to find out how the thing works.'

He picked up a damp cloth and wiped the smudge carefully from her face and she reached up and kissed him. 'There, that's better,' he said. As she poured coffee into two mugs he leaned back against the door and lit a cigarette.

'Here's your coffee, darling,' she said and handed him a mug. At the same moment she noticed the holstered gun on his hip. 'Oh, Mark! Do you expect trouble so soon?' she said anxiously.

He raised a reassuring hand. 'Don't go getting flustered,' he said. 'I always expect trouble in these waters. We're not far from Bias Bay which is crawling with pirates – some of them led by women.'

She laughed and threw back her head. 'You're kidding me.'

He shook his head. 'No, I'm in deadly earnest. If you happen to be on deck and you notice any innocent-looking motor sampans or junks call me quickly. They have a nasty habit of sailing close and suddenly about a hundred men appear on deck, all screaming for blood.'

She cut sandwiches as he talked and he watched her over the rim of his mug. She was wearing old denims and a polo-necked sweater and somehow managed to look more feminine than ever. The memory of what had happened that afternoon suddenly came into his mind and he felt acutely uncomfortable. He put down the mug and said: 'I've got things to do. I'll see you later. Don't forget to get plenty of sleep.'

He went down to the engine-room and found O'Hara oiling various parts of the engine in the pale, oil-sick light of an inspection lamp. The noise was so deafening that he had to tap the old man on the shoulder and point upwards with his thumb. They scrambled up on deck and Hagen said, 'Everything all right?'

'Fine,' the old man said. 'Those engines will run from now till Domesday.'

'Good, I've decided to increase to top speed now.'

O'Hara's eyes widened in surprise. 'But I thought you wanted to maintain a constant speed,' he said. 'You worked it all out.'

Hagen nodded. 'Yes, I know, but I've been thinking. If we maintain a cruising speed we'll pass through the Hainan Straits about noon tomorrow. There's usually a lot of light naval craft around there and a small boat like ours would excite their damned curiosity. Another thing; what if Kossoff has alerted the Red naval base at Kiung Chow on Hainan Island? He's a smart man. He'd give them orders to let us through but to tip him off that we were on the way. That's no good. I want to take the bastard by surprise.'

'O'Hara nodded. 'Sounds fine to me but what about the rest of the trip? We can't approach the marshes in daylight.'

Hagen nodded. 'We won't need to. After we're through the straits I'll reduce speed and we can take it easy tomorrow.'

O'Hara suddenly exploded with laughter and took out his pipe. 'My God, but 'tis a hell of a thing we're trying to get away with this time, lad, and I'm only just beginning to realize it. Ah, well. They say the divil looks after his own.'

Hagen went into the wheelhouse and told Mason to increase speed and then he went down to the cabin and flopped down on his bunk. He lay staring at the bulkhead and thinking about the gold and the marshes and the girl. He could hear a low rumble of voices from the galley and knew that O'Hara must be sampling some of Rose's coffee. Once she laughed quite distinctly and he found himself smiling with her and then the sound of the voices began to merge with the throb of the engine and the splashing of the sea.

He was not conscious of having slept, only of being suddenly awake and looking at his watch and realizing, with a sense of shock, that it was three in the morning. He pulled on a heavy reefer coat and as he buttoned it up around his throat he heard a grunt as someone turned in his sleep. He struck a match and discovered Mason, a sardonic quirk on his lips even in sleep. He quietly left the cabin and went up on deck.

There was a slight sea-mist lifting off the

water and *Hurrier* was kicking along at a tremendous pace. There was no moon but the night sky was a jewel-studded delight and there was still that peculiar luminosity to the water. He walked along the heaving deck and opened the glass-panelled door of the wheel-house. O'Hara was standing at the wheel and a fine, weird figure he cut. The only illumination was the compass light which, being directly beneath his face, shone upwards, so that the first hurried impression was of a disembodied face floating five and a half feet above the ground. 'How are things going?' Hagen said.

'Couldn't be better. You'd think the old girl had an engagement with a gentleman at the other end, the way she's lifting along.'

As he slipped to one side to allow Hagen to take over the wheel there was a distinct aroma of rum. For a moment anger welled in Hagen and then he restrained it. After all, the old man had done a good day's work. As O'Hara went out Hagen called: 'Go easy on that rum. I don't want you starting a jag.'

'Now you know you can depend on me,

lad,' O'Hara said in a hurt voice. He moved away along the deck whistling a sadly gay little jig.

Hagen put a cigarette in his mouth and, pulling a hinged seat down from the wall, settled his back comfortably and sat holding the wheel lightly in his hands, watching the foam curl alongside the prow. Occasionally, spray spattered against the windows and gradually his mind wandered away on old and long-forgotten paths. He thought of incidents and people long since past with a sort of measured sadness. This was a period he looked forward to on a voyage. To be alone with the sea and the night and the boat. It was as if the world did not exist. During such quiet spaces time had no meaning and an hour had the habit of passing like a minute. He checked his watch and saw that it was ten past four. The door opened softly, coinciding with a spatter of rain against the windows. He smelt the aroma of coffee, heavy on the morning air, and there was another more subtle fragrance that by now he was so well accustomed to. 'What's wrong with bed at this time in the morning?' he asked her.

She chuckled. 'The first real chance to be alone together and the man asks silly questions. Is there anywhere I can sit?' He pulled down another seat for her and she settled herself. She handed him a mug of coffee. 'Like a sandwich?'

They ate in a companionable and intimate silence, their knees touching. Afterwards he gave her a cigarette and they smoked and talked quietly as rain hammered forcefully against the window. After one particular interlude of silence she said, 'You love the sea, don't you?'

He considered the point and then answered: 'I suppose I do. You see for me it's always been a refuge, whether I was running as a boy from my father's anger to the sailing dinghy I sailed on the sound in Connecticut, or standing out to sea in *Hurrier* from some unwelcome port. The sea is home in a way. She's rather like a woman, capricious, unreliable, at times even cruel and treacherous, but that doesn't mean you love her any the less or that she ceases to fascinate.'

Rose laughed from the darkness. 'Thank you for the extremely apt analogy. There are hidden depths in you.'

He grinned wryly. 'The secret soul of Mark Hagen. I'm getting sentimental in my old age.' He swivelled to the small chart table and switched on a tiny, hooded light. He checked his calculations again and said: 'Well, angel, unless I miss my guess we should be entering the Straits of Hainan within the next fifteen minutes. Should be pretty tricky.'

'Shall I wake the others?'

He shook his head. 'No, they wouldn't be able to help.' He strained his eyes through the darkness and, as for a brief moment the rain lifted, he thought he could see Hainan. 'I want you to look to starboard,' he told her, 'and keep looking. The starboard side of the straits is formed by the Lui-Chow Peninsula. There should be a lighthouse but you know what the Commies are like – still, it might be working.'

They continued at full throttle for half an hour and Hagen knew that they must be well into the straits by now. The inference was obvious. The lighthouse lamp was out. Suddenly to port he saw a lighthouse and several lights, like a string of yellow beads thrown down carelessly, and then the rain curtain dropped back into place and hid them from sight. His spirits lifted. 'Everything's fine,' he told the girl. 'That was Kiung Chow, a port on Hainan. We're dead on course.'

'Now what?' she said.

'Now we sit tight and go like a bat out of hell for about an hour and a half and then look for a light to starboard. Thank God for this weather. It really gives us a sporting chance.'

The engines throbbed steadily and the rain continued to spatter against the windows. After a while Rose dozed off, her head lolling against his shoulder. Hagen continued on the alert, his eyes piercing the darkness until they were sore and he had difficulty in keeping them open. At six-fifteen he prodded her into life and told her to watch for a light on the starboard side. Within five minutes she had found it, a tiny pin-point piercing the dark. 'That's Cape Kami light,' he told her. 'We're nearly through. We should pass Lamko Point light to port in about ten minutes and then our troubles will be over.'

It was as though everything was happening according to a predestined plan. Lamko Point winked at them through the rain right on schedule and Hagen altered course at once. For another twenty minutes they ploughed on through the darkness and then he reduced speed and leaned back with a sigh of relief. 'That's it, angel,' he said. 'We're through.'

She squeezed his arm and said, 'What happens now?'

He laughed shortly. 'Now, we just take it easy all day and pray nobody spots us before nightfall.'

The rain gradually stopped and dawn began to seep into the sky. Quite suddenly it was daylight with a slight mist on the sea and a chill wind but Hagen hardly noticed the cold. He opened one of the windows and the day had a sweetness like sharp wine and he felt drunk with its beauty. He looked at Rose and was suddenly aware, with a sense of shock, of the tiredness and strain that showed in her eyes. 'Are you all right?' he asked.

She tried to smile and then her face cracked into despair and fear. 'Oh, Mark, I'll be glad when it's over. Oh, God, make it be over soon.' She turned quickly and wrenched open the door and disappeared along the deck. For a moment Hagen stood staring at the open door that swung to and fro as the boat dipped into the waves and then the cold morning wind cut into him and he was afraid. For the first time he was really and truly afraid.

Mason relieved him at eight o'clock and Hagen went down to his cabin and turned in. He slept well without dreaming and didn't even raise his head until O'Hara came to wake him at three o'clock. O'Hara did his trick at the wheel while Rose gave Hagen and Mason a meal. She didn't have a great deal to say and still looked very tired. Hagen noticed Mason following her with his eyes as she passed in and out of the cabin. The bitter and sardonic lines on his face were momentarily wiped away until he caught Hagen looking at him and he flushed angrily.

It was after the meal, when Hagen had relieved O'Hara, that Mason came to the wheelhouse. He closed the door and leaned against it, a cigarette smouldering between his lips. Hagen had been expecting such a visit. He waited for the big man to make his proposition and found that he didn't hate Mason half as much as he had imagined. Mason said, 'I think it's time you and I had a little chat, don't you?'

'What's on your mind?' Hagen said.

Mason blew out a perfect smoke ring. 'When Charlie told me I was going on this trip I wasn't very cheerful at first and then I heard the details and got interested. You see I began to realize that there were very distinct possibilities.' Hagen laughed harshly and Mason said, 'What's so funny?'

'You are. Let me finish for you. You'll now point out to me what fools we would be to ever go back to Charlie at all. Why not go to Saigon, you'll say, and keep all the profits.'

Mason relaxed again. 'So you're a mind-reader? What's wrong with the idea? You're going to twist the girl, aren't you?'

Anger ran hotly through Hagen's veins and then he pulled himself up sharply. Mason was only telling the truth. 'That's nothing to do with it,' he told Mason. 'We need Charlie to dispose of the gold for us. In Saigon it would take time. He'd be breathing down our necks within twenty-four hours.'

Mason straightened up and said coldly: 'I don't give a damn for Charlie or you or anybody. Everything I've ever done has gone sour on me. This is my last chance. I warn you, if that gold comes out of the marshes, I want a share.' He ground his cigarette viciously into the floor and said: 'If we don't get out of the marshes – then we lose. It's as simple as that. I might as well be dead as end up another drifter on the Macao waterfront.' He opened the door and went out.

Hagen watched him walk along to the prow where Rose was sunning herself lying on a blanket. He dropped down beside her and they began to talk. Hagen was disturbed at the curious parallel between Mason and himself. In many ways they were identical and now they were both at the end of the road. The last big chance.

He stayed at the wheel until six o'clock when Mason came to relieve him and he went below for some food. Rose looked considerably better and a lot of the strain had disappeared from around her eyes. There was no sign of O'Hara. 'Where's the old man?' Hagen asked her.

She looked surprised. 'I thought you must have given him a job to do in the engine-room. I haven't seen him for ages.'

Hagen sighed wearily and stood up. What a crew, he thought. A girl, a deserter and a rum-soaked old has-been. He cursed savagely and went along to the engine-room. He found O'Hara huddled against the bottom of the ladder, dead to the world. The stink of rum was appalling and there were two empty bottles lying at the old man's feet. Hagen lifted him like a sack of potatoes and pushed him up through the hatch on to the deck. Rose looked concerned. 'Is he sick?' she said anxiously.

'He's sick all right,' Hagen said. He threw

a bucket on a line overboard and doused the old man with sea water. After a few moments he seemed to be coming round. 'Watch him for a minute, angel,' Hagen said and slipped down into the engine-room. He had the over-developed cunning of the habitual drunk to overcome, but long practice in dealing with O'Hara now came to his aid. He checked all the unlikely places and finally found an oil drum that sounded hollow. He pulled off the lid and discovered a large cardboard box lined with bottles.

He carried the heavy box up the ladder and dropped it down by the stern rail. He lifted a couple of bottles out and examined them. A cheap rot-gut masquerading under a fancy name and guaranteed to produce cirrhosis of the liver in half the usual time. He began to drop the bottles overboard one by one. O'Hara came to his senses enough to realize what was happening and struggled to his feet. 'No, lad! Not that! Not all of them.'

Hagen turned and said coldly: 'I warned you about this. Now you'll have to suffer. I'll keep two bottles and you'll have a swig when I say so. The rest goes over.' He handed two bottles to Rose and then lifted the box and dropped it overboard.

O'Hara jumped at his back, screaming something unintelligible, his gnarled old fingers clawing at Hagen's throat. Hagen swung round and jerked the old man away. He slapped him several times across the face. 'Now less of it and pull yourself together,' he said.

O'Hara was blubbering like a baby and when Hagen released his grip on his shirt front he slid to the deck, his body shaking convulsively. Rose dropped to her knees and put an arm around him. She looked up at Hagen, pain on her face. 'Was that necessary? He's an old man you know.'

As Hagen tried to think of a suitable reply the engines were cut and the boat began to slow down. Mason's voice rang through the unaccustomed stillness. 'Yes, he's an old man, Hagen. Why don't you try someone a little nearer your own age?'

The challenge was unmistakable. He looked big and competent and very sure of himself with the sun glinting in his fair hair. Hagen waved a hand invitingly at the open deck between them and Mason moved forward, lightly, like a cat poised for action. He looked supremely confident.

Hagen pulled off his cap and wiped the sweat from his brow and stood waiting. He felt curiously detached from the affair. The challenge had to be met, he realized that. The success of everything depended on it. It wasn't a chivalrous action on Mason's part in defence of an old man. It was a heaven-sent opportunity to destroy Hagen that he had seized on as it presented itself.

The man looked like a boxer and as he approached he lifted his balled fists and assumed a classic pose. Hagen had no fear. He almost welcomed the fight. This was something concrete to deal with, not abstract. As Mason swung the first punch, Hagen grabbed his wrist and twisted in one of his favourite Judo throws. The next moment he found himself flying through the air to land with terrible force on the deck. His throw had been expertly countered.

Mason stood back, a smile on his face, and flexed his hands. 'Get up, you bastard,' he said. 'I'm just beginning to enjoy myself.'

Hagen got to his feet and leaned against the deck-house. There was a mist before his eyes and he had no strength left in him at all. As Mason moved towards him he turned and staggered away along the side of the deck-house. He felt sick and faint and behind him he could hear the roar of anger from Mason. He knew if he didn't do something drastic he'd be pounded into the deck within the next few seconds. He stumbled round the corner of the deck-house and suddenly flung himself down so that Mason, who was following hard behind, tripped over him and crashed to the deck. Hagen stood up and began to kick him methodically in the stomach and suddenly there was a great roaring in his ears that deafened him to everything except the one purpose. To smash Mason into the deck.

Through the roaring he heard a voice screaming: 'Stop it, Mark! You'll kill him!' And then hands dragged him away. He remembered staggering into the cabin and holding on to the table in an effort to retain his senses, and then the cabin floor heaved towards him and he dived into darkness.

His head was in her lap and she was crying and cleaning his face gently with a damp cloth. As he stirred and lifted his head she said frantically: 'Oh, Mark. Are you all right? Say something, please.'

Surprisingly he discovered that his mouth retained its original shape but one side of his face was considerably swollen where it had met the deck. He tried to grin. 'I bet I look a hell of a sight.'

She sobbed with relief. 'Thank God! For the last half hour I've been nearly out of my mind.'

He struggled to his feet and stood swaying, supporting himself on the table. 'I'm sorry you had to see that,' he said.

'I thought you were going to kill him.'

He raised an eyebrow. 'What do you think he was trying to do to me?'

He stumbled out on to the deck in time to see Mason struggle to his feet and vomit. The big man stood swaying for a moment, as if he might topple over again, and then he tossed the canvas bucket, on its line, into the sea and washed away the vomit with a vigorous spray of water. 'Always the gentleman,' Hagen said.

Mason turned towards him. His face wasn't too good and his lips were split. He grinned without rancour. 'Another time, Hagen.' He stripped his shirt away, exposing the livid bruises on his stomach and chest, and dived cleanly over the rail and broke into an effortless crawl.

Hagen pulled his sweat shirt over his head and followed him over the rail. The water was warm but refreshing and the salt got into his cuts and grazes stinging him into life again. After a few minutes he shouted to Mason and then returned to the boat and pulled himself back over the rail. Rose handed him a towel and he dried himself briskly and pulled on his shirt. 'Your pants are still wet,' she pointed out.

He grinned and suddenly felt very tender towards her. 'You can never stop acting like a woman,' he said. 'You're all the same.' She pouted and as Mason climbed over the rail,

Hagen added, 'I'll get the boat moving again now the performance is over.'

Mason grinned at him and went below and Rose said, 'I'll bring you a cup of coffee in a few minutes.' Hagen nodded and went back to the wheelhouse. Within a few moments *Hurrier* was sliding rapidly through the water again.

It was exactly ten o'clock when he cut the engines and the boat glided forward silently for a little while before coming to a halt. The other three were all on deck and Mason had one of the sub-machine-guns cradled in his arms ready for action. Not more than a quarter of a mile through the darkness the Kwai Marshes waited for them and Hagen's palms began to sweat a little as he prepared for the most difficult part of the journey.

He had charted a course into the marshes by a little-known channel he had once used when running guns in to the Reds. He was banking on the fact that Kossoff would be waiting for him at the river mouth if indeed he was waiting at all. He would never imagine that a boat could enter the marshes by any

other route. Fog was rolling from the land
in patches and he could smell the foetid odour
of the marshes that was carried towards them
on the stiff, off-shore breeze. They all waited,
poised and tense, ears strained for every
sound.

There was only the lapping of the water
against the hull and the sighing of the wind.
Hagen pressed the starter and the engine
roared into life, shattering the stillness of the
night. He hurriedly throttled down until they
were moving in towards the marshes at a
steady five knots, the engine rumbling protestingly on a low note.

There was sweat trickling down his face
now as the shape of the land moved out of
the night towards them, but there were no
shots fired, no alarms. Nothing to indicate
that Kossoff was anywhere within a thousand
miles. Hagen took the boat through several
twisting channels and cut the engines and ran
her gently in amongst the giant reeds. He
emitted a slow whistle of relief and went out
on deck. 'Well, what now?' Mason said.

'So far so good. We've got in – let's hope

169

we can get out as easily when the time comes. We've a big day tomorrow. I think everybody should turn in.'

'What about a guard?' Mason said.

Hagen told him then that he would take first watch and Mason nodded, and he and O'Hara went below. Rose lingered for a brief moment. Hagen held her hand for a little while without saying anything and then she kissed him quickly and followed the others.

He sat back in the wheelhouse, smoking and nursing a sub-machine-gun, and he smelled the marsh all around and heard the crickets singing through the night, and for the first time he began to think that there might be a chance – just a chance – that everything would go off without a hitch.

8

He was awakened shortly before seven the
next morning by Mason who told him he
had just been relieved by O'Hara who was
keeping a sober, if rather bleary, eye on their
surroundings. Rose was up and already
preparing breakfast. Hagen swallowed a cup
of coffee and went on deck and told O'Hara
to go below and get some breakfast. He
climbed on top of the wheelhouse and looked
around him.

As he considered the wide expanse of reeds,
he reflected with satisfaction that nowhere
could there be a better place in which to play
hide-and-seek. Some distance away the China
Sea was hazy in the morning sun and inland

the reeds seemed to continue unbroken as far as the eye could see.

Hagen knew that this was not so. Interlaced among the reeds was a network of waterways and lagoons – some deep, some shallow. He also knew that somewhere deep in the marshes people lived. Primitive fishermen who built their houses either on piles or the occasional islands. He had met some of these people on previous visits, simple and hard-working, wresting a living from their difficult surroundings. For them there was no Nationalist or Communist Government; the outside world had no meaning for them and they continued to live in the fever and the heat, toiling for their living as they had done for a thousand years.

A flight of wildfowl lifted from the reeds nearby and curved away towards the sea. He dropped down on to the deck and shouted for the others. They all came up from the galley and followed him into the wheelhouse. He pulled out the chart and gave them the full picture. 'From now on it's going to be tough,' he said. 'We've got to be on our toes and ready for trouble at any time of the day or night. There may be scouts out looking for us and we're pretty certain to bump into some of the primitive fishermen who live in the marshes. I don't think we need worry about them. They don't know a Communist from a tax-collector.'

Mason interrupted impatiently. 'Okay, Hagen! But what about the gold? How long will it take us to get to it?'

Hagen frowned and said: 'That's the trouble. According to the cross-bearing Rose has given me we're only eight miles from the lagoon in which the launch sank. As you can see from this chart all the water-ways in the marshes aren't marked. In other words, we might have to go through twenty miles of waterway to get to our destination.'

Mason snorted his disbelief. 'Hell, it can't be that bad.'

Hagen smiled grimly. 'I know this place. You'll be up to your waist in mud and pushing before we're through.' Mason still looked unconvinced and Hagen rolled up the map and said, 'The sooner we get started the sooner we'll be there.'

The rest of the morning was a nightmare. The stench from the marshes coupled with the furnace heat of the sun sapped their strength and for the first two or three miles they had to push and haul the boat through what could only be described as liquid mud. At two o'clock, after five hours of sweat and agony, they came out into a broad waterway and Hagen called a halt for rest and food.

Tempers had noticeably frayed and nobody seemed to have much appetite. The mosquitoes were beginning to be a nuisance and the repellent cream which Rose had discovered in the first-aid box didn't seem to affect them much. Rose looked particularly washed-out. All morning she had toiled with the rest of them and the labour had obviously affected her frail body. Mason's face was blotched with insect bites and the cuts and bruises left by the fight looked particularly unhealthy. 'How much longer of this?' he demanded. 'It's bloody murder.'

Hagen shrugged. 'I warned you,' he said. 'Anyway, with luck things may be easier. Let's hope this channel goes in the right direction.'

He went into the wheelhouse and pressed the starter and took the boat forward at a slow speed.

He carefully steered along the winding course, occasionally turning into tributaries to keep the correct compass bearing. It was almost with surprise that he took the boat into a broad lagoon one and a half hours later and cut the engines. 'This is it,' he announced.

There was an excited babble of sound from his three companions. Rose stood at the rail, a hand shielding her eyes from the sun, and slowly pivoted, her eyes covering the entire lagoon. Her shoulders drooped. 'This isn't it,' she said.

Mason cursed. 'Are you sure, Rose?'

She nodded. 'It was much smaller than this and completely surrounded by reeds. I remember my father running the boat into the reeds to hide her and then we suddenly came out into this small lagoon. It was pretty dark but I remember quite clearly.'

Hagen climbed up on top of the wheelhouse and looked around. He could see nothing, only the reeds stretching away into the distance. He jumped down on to the deck and started to peel off his shirt. 'There's nothing for it,' he said to Mason. 'We'll have to go for a swim.'

Mason grinned and began to undress. 'We're certainly having to do things the hard way on this trip,' he said.

Mason went over the side and struck off in one direction and Hagen smiled confidently to Rose and said: 'Don't worry, angel. We'll find your secret lagoon.' He vaulted over the side and started to swim in the opposite direction to Mason.

The water wasn't as bad as he had expected. It smelled a trifle earthy but not offensively so and the coolness was a pleasant relief after the heat. He swam into a narrow lane that cut into the reeds and followed its course for several yards. When it came to a dead end he swam into the reeds themselves. It was easier than he had expected, and within a few seconds he came out into a small lagoon. For a moment his spirits rose and then disappointment came. The water was quite shallow and clear to a sandy bottom and there was no sunken launch. He turned back into the reeds and swam in another direction.

Every so often he hailed the boat and heard Rose's clear voice replying, and in this way he managed to keep a sense of direction. Now and then he could hear Mason's voice in the distance but he seemed to be having no better luck. After half an hour he began to tire and followed the sound of the girl's voice until, finally, he came out into the lagoon again. Mason was already on board and gave him a hand up. They sat smoking cigarettes and Mason said, 'He couldn't have been that far out when he took his bearings, could he?'

Hagen tried to look cheerful. 'No, it must be around here somewhere,' he said, and inside he was thinking of a dying man on a sinking boat in the dusk. He tossed his cigarette into the water and followed it over the side. Mason struck off in an entirely new direction and Hagen started to swim to the far end of the lagoon which seemed to be halted by a thick barrier of reeds. He forced his way in through the reeds for about fifty feet and then decided to go back. Afterwards he was never sure why he decided to go a little further. The important thing was that he did and found himself on the edge of a small lagoon, roughly circular in shape and perhaps a hundred feet in diameter. The water was clear as glass and the bottom was white sand, the mud scoured clean away. It shelved steeply towards the centre and as he started to swim forward he felt afraid. In the other parts of the marsh the air was full of the clamour of a thousand living things but here not even the crickets sang. For a moment he shivered as he remembered stories he had heard as a child of fairy pools back home in Ireland, and then he said softly, 'Don't be a bloody fool,' and kept on swimming.

It was as if he was the first person ever to enter that place but he was not. He had known in his heart from the beginning that this was the place. He floated motionless, not far from the centre of the lagoon, and looked down at the launch for a moment, and then he took a deep breath and did a steep surface dive that carried him down through the clear water.

He could feel the pressure in his ears and swallowed a couple of times until it eased off and then he was hanging on to the deck-rail of the launch. He stayed there for a moment and had a quick look at the condition of the wreck and then he released his grip on the rail and shot to the surface.

As he came out into the bright sunlight and trod water, taking deep breaths of fresh air, he realized to his surprise that in front of him floated a roughly made canoe and sitting in it was a Chinese fisherman who looked as if he had just received the fright of his life. Hagen reached the canoe in one easy stroke and smiled and said: 'Do not fear. I am a man as you are.'

An expression of relief came to the fisherman's face. He spoke Cantonese in a debased form but Hagen found that he could follow it with reasonable ease. 'Praise the gods you are a man for I thought you were one of the water-devils that live in this evil place.'

Hagen pulled himself over the prow of the frail canoe and sat in the bottom. 'I come from a large boat over there,' he said, pointing through the reeds. 'Will you take me to it?'

The fisherman nodded and pointed down to the launch. 'This is an evil place and a water-devil lives in the wreck. It is death to dive in this place.'

'But I have just done it and lived,' Hagen pointed out.

The man considered the point and nodded wisely. 'Then the devil must be sleeping.'

They paused at the edge of the reeds and Hagen said, 'If it is such an evil place why do you come?'

Grief darkened the fisherman's face as he explained. He and his brother had discovered the launch, and his brother had insisted on diving. The launch must have been in a certain state of balance. Apparently it had heeled over while the brother was in the cabin and he had been trapped and drowned. Hagen had noticed a mass of damaged superstructure blocking the cabin door. This explained the unhappy man's fate. The simple explanation was not accepted by the fisherman who saw in the incident the action of a water-devil.

'The reason for his visits lay in his great sorrow, for his brother's soul was for ever imprisoned in his body unless it was recovered. Only a resting place in the earth of the tribal burial island assured a soul of an after life.

As they came out through the reeds into the large lagoon Hagen said, 'I intend to dive again to the wreck and I shall recover your brother's body.'

The man placed a hand to his mouth in a gesture of awe. 'I do not think you are an ordinary man if you can do this thing, lord.' He bowed slightly. 'Your humble servant Chang whose people will do anything in their power to help you.'

They paddled up to the boat and Rose and O'Hara leaned over the side in surprise. 'I've found it,' Hagen said. 'Just as you described it, angel.' Mason was hailed and came swimming out of the reeds to join them.

Hagen sat on the deck with Chang and questioned him closely. Yes, he had seen white men before. They sometimes came and met other boats. Many large boxes changed

181

hands. Mason couldn't understand Cantonese and interrupted with ill-concealed impatience. 'He's seen gun-runners in here before but not for a long time,' Hagen explained. He asked Chang if there had been strangers in the marshes within the last few days. The fisherman shook his head. There had been no one. They would have known. They could always tell when strangers came.

Hagen stood up and stretched. He felt satisfied. Very satisfied. It looked as though they were ahead of Kossoff all along the line. A sudden decision came to him and he turned into the wheelhouse. A moment later the engine roared into life and the boat gathered speed and crashed into the reeds at the end of the lagoon. For a moment the reeds seemed an impossible barrier and then they slowly parted. *Hurrier* passed through into the small lagoon and Hagen cut the engines. He ran to the prow quickly and threw out the anchor. Mason and the others watched him in amazement. 'What the hell's got into you?' Mason said.

Hagen laughed excitedly and said to

Chang: 'You must stay until sunset. I shall have your brother's body for you then.' He went into the cabin and reappeared dragging the box that contained his diving gear.

Rose made a sudden exclamation. 'You aren't diving tonight, Mark?' He nodded and began to lay out his equipment in orderly rows. She turned to Mason and said wildly: 'Stop him, Steve! Make him listen to reason.'

Mason said: 'You've had a hell of a day, Hagen. What's the rush? We've got all day tomorrow. We know the stuff is down there.'

Hagen pulled on rubber flippers and explained. 'Don't you see? Kossoff hasn't arrived yet. That means we've been one jump ahead of him all the time. I want to keep it that way. There's a body in the cabin down there and the entrance is blocked. I want them both cleared tonight and then we can start to raise the gold first thing in the morning.'

He hoisted the aqua-lung on to his back and O'Hara fastened it into place for him. Mason looked up at the sky and said: 'I think you're wasting your time. It'll be sunset in an hour and a half.'

Hagen ignored him and said to O'Hara: 'Get that block and tackle rigged up as quickly as possible. I may need it.' He adjusted his diving-mask and gripped the mouthpiece of his breathing-tube firmly between his teeth. As he moved to the rail he heard Rose give a protesting cry and then he vaulted over the side, down into the clear water.

For a moment he paused to adjust the flow of oxygen and then he swam down in a long sweeping curve. The sensation of floating in space, alone in a silent world, fascinated him as always and it was with a feeling of elation that he approached the wreck. At once he realized the position was more difficult than he had appreciated. The launch was almost bottom up. She had heeled right over on the sloping bottom and a portion of the cabin roof, apparently severely damaged in the fight with the gunboat, had been pressed in a tangled mass down over the entrance to the cabin. He hovered for a few minutes over the wreckage and made a few tentative attempts at dislodging some of the twisted metal, but he could see at once that he was wasting his time. He kicked upwards towards the surface and emerged into the evening sunlight astern of *Hurrier*.

Mason reached down and hauled him aboard and Hagen pulled off his diving-mask and asked for a cigarette. 'How does it look?' Mason asked.

Hagen fingered the cigarette thoughtfully. 'Not so good,' he said and proceeded to explain: 'From what I can see there must be two currents of water emptying into this lagoon. That's how it's got the circular shape. They've scoured away the mud and sand between them. The bottom shelves at quite an angle to the centre and the launch was resting at an acute angle when Chang's brother entered the cabin. I think he must have dislodged something inside and the launch has heeled over until most of the cabin roof is rammed down against the bottom of the lagoon. It's a damaged portion of the roof that seems to be blocking the door.'

Rose nodded. 'The roof *was* damaged. Cannon shell, I think.'

Mason grunted and said, 'Well, what now?'

Hagen grinned. 'I'll blast it open. It's a damned good job Charlie produced that plastic waterproof explosive.'

Mason shrugged and said: 'Okay, Hagen. You're the boss.' He brought the blasting equipment up from the cabin while Hagen hauled up the anchor and O'Hara started the engines and moved *Hurrier* to the edge of the lagoon.

As they prepared the charges Mason said: 'Do you think we've moved far enough? No good blasting ourselves as well.'

Hagen, nodded. 'It's a small charge,' he said. 'I only want to open the launch up – not blow the thing apart.'

He adjusted his diving equipment and went over the side again carrying the prepared charges and detonators and wire. He could not see as clearly as he would have liked and he realized that dusk was falling fast. He laid two charges at strategic points amongst the tangled mass that blocked the cabin door and wired them up. He worked fast and returned to the surface within a few minutes, the wire clutched firmly in one hand. He sat on deck feeling suddenly very tired, and Mason said, 'How was it?'

Hagen grinned tiredly. 'Not so bad. Visibility is beginning to get poor, though.' He nodded to O'Hara who depressed the plunger of the detonating box. The water heaved and there was a dull roar and *Hurrier* rocked violently as the surface of the lagoon was disturbed. After a few moments wreckage began to float to the surface of the water and kept coming up for about fifteen minutes. They watched in silence and gradually the shadows deepened as the sky turned to gold and crimson far out over the sea.

The water was cloudy with mud and sand and Rose said: 'You can't go down again, Mark. You won't be able to see a thing.'

For a moment Hagen almost gave in and then the stubbornness that was the essential core of his nature took control. 'Bring me the lamp,' he told O'Hara. He turned to Rose and said, with a weary smile: 'I've dived at night many a time. You have to when it's someone else's pearling ground.'

O'Hara appeared from the wheelhouse

with the lamp, a large, powerful spot on a long cable, which plugged into the boat's lighting system and was specially designed for underwater use. Hagen carried the lamp in one hand and a crowbar in the other when he dived again.

The beam thrown out by the lamp was very powerful and he saw the wreck almost all the way down, and for some reason it looked sinister and ghostly. Perhaps it was just that he was tired, he thought, and just the slightest bit light-headed, but as he poised over the wreck he felt afraid. The launch was still tilted over at the same crazy angle, but in place of the tangled mass of wreckage was now a gaping black hole. He floated down and shone his lamp into the cabin but could see nothing. For a moment he hesitated and then, holding the lamp in front of him, he ventured into the interior.

He shone the lamp into each corner of the cabin but saw nothing unusual. It was a strange sensation to be floating with the ceiling beneath his feet and the floor above his head. There was a door to another cabin in front of him and he swam towards it and immediately his spotlight touched upon a jumble of bricks and broken boxes that lay in a heap in the angle of the wall and the ceiling. The gold! There it was, the reality after all the dreaming, and then he was aware of a movement out of the corner of his eye. He swung the beam upwards, illuminating all the cabin, and saw with horror a man walking towards him, arms extended. Hagen screamed soundlessly and struck out with the crowbar and the figure bounced away to the other side of the cabin and hovered there.

Chang's brother! Hagen suddenly felt weak and faint. In his state of exhausion and under the eerie conditions it had seemed as if the water-devil Chang had spoken of had existed in reality. Some freak of nature had caused the gases in his body to suspend him upright like a living man. He was a ghastly sight, bloated and horrible, and Hagen had to summon up his last reserves of will-power and guts to swim over and grip him by the hair. He kept his face turned away and swam out of the cabin, towing the body behind him.

It was quite a struggle. The body got stuck in the jagged opening, and he had to turn back and wrestle with it to get it through. It was funny how he kept thinking of it as a person and not as an inanimate thing. He gripped it round the waist and pulled it clear of the wreck. The spongy feel of the flesh sickened him and he released his grip. The gas-filled body shot up to the surface, glowing with a sort of phosphorescence, and he followed it up slowly.

He bumped against the side of *Hurrier* and eager hands reached over and pulled him aboard. He lay on the deck and allowed them to divest him of his equipment and wrap him in a blanket. It was almost dark but he was able to see that Rose was extremely pale as she leaned over him. 'Did it come up?' he asked.

She nodded, lips compressed, and Mason said: 'Did it come up? It almost shot out of the water. It scared the living daylights out of me.'

O'Hara said, 'Well, there he goes,' and Hagen struggled to his feet and saw Chang paddling towards the reeds, his brother's body floating behind the canoe, secured by a cord.

The fisherman turned and waved from the gloom. 'I shall return tomorrow, lord,' he said and then disappeared into the reeds.

Hagen started to limp towards the cabin door and then he remembered something. He turned and said, with a grimace: 'I almost forgot. It's there – the gold I mean. Just waiting to be lifted. Shouldn't take more than a couple of hours.'

As he turned and stumbled down into the cabin an excited babble of sound broke out behind him. He flopped on to the bed, completely and utterly exhausted, so that he had not even the strength to cover himself with the blankets. He lay with a cigarette, thinking, and as things began to blur, the cigarette was taken from between his fingers and blankets were carefully tucked in around his body. For a moment cool lips touched his and he inhaled her fragrance and then there was nothing.

9

Hagen came awake quickly from a deep and dreamless sleep. It was as though he had come into existence at the moment his eyes opened, and he lay in the semi-darkness of the cabin and wondered who he was. It was no new sensation, this. He had experienced it often during the war and always it had followed a period of great stress and mental strain. For the two or three minutes that the feeling lasted he felt very bad and then he relaxed completely as he remembered.

He slipped from the bunk and stood shivering, his feet cold on the cabin floor. Mason and O'Hara slept soundly, the old man gently snoring, and he quietly opened the door and went out on deck.

He stood at the rail and gazed at the lagoon, now shrouded in early morning mist. He made a swift decision and gently lowered himself over the rail. The water was cold on first contact and he swallowed a howl in his throat and swam quietly across to the reeds. After a few minutes he returned to the boat and hauled himself back over the rail. There was a towel lying on the deck and as he looked at it in puzzlement Rose came out of the cabin with a coffee-pot and two mugs. ''Morning,' she said softly. 'How did you sleep?'

'Not so bad,' he said. He towelled down briskly as she poured the coffee. His body was still bruised and marked from his fight with Mason and he had not shaved since Macao. 'You look quite rugged and dangerous,' she told him, handing him his coffee.

He slipped the towel over his shoulders and sat down on the engine-room hatch. 'Like a man out of Hemingway?' he said.

She chuckled and a smile wrinkled her

nose. She sat beside him and gazed at the morning with a happy expression on her face. 'Oh, it's good to be alive.'

For the first time he was really and truly moved by her. It was not a physical desire, it was something inimical. Something of such depth that it frightened him. He suddenly felt that the time had come for complete honesty between them. He fumbled with the mug and began awkwardly: 'Rose, there's something I want you to know. Something we've got to get straight.'

She turned her head towards him and her lips were slightly parted as she waited for him to speak and then a voice said: 'Well! Well! Early birds!' Mason walked out of the cabin.

He sat down beside them on the hatch and Rose said, 'I'll get another cup.'

Mason offered Hagen a cigarette and as he lit it, said: 'Am I mistaken or did I interrupt something? Have you told her?'

'I was going to tell her as you came in.'

Mason nodded and said thoughtfully, 'Are you still going to tell her?'

Hagen started to say yes and then he suddenly knew that the moment had passed. He sighed and cursed softly. 'No, it will have to wait a little while longer.'

Mason laughed and there was sympathy in his voice. 'You know I feel sorry for you, Hagen. From being the white-haired boy you're going to become the worst heel she's ever met.' He slapped him on the shoulder. 'Come on. Let's get breakfast over and we can start the diving.'

For a moment Hagen lingered on deck. He could hear Mason greet Rose with a joke and she laughed gaily, and he cursed softly to himself because he knew that Mason was right. For the moment he decided to leave the situation as it was and went down into the cabin.

It was nine-thirty when Hagen made the first dive and by that time the sun was high in the sky and visibility under water was crystal-clear. He poised over the launch, looking her over, and laughed to himself when he thought of his fears of the previous evening. The sunlight streamed through the water and coloured fish swam in and around the launch. He swam down and entered through the shattered entrance to the cabin. Sunlight streamed down through the crystal water and in through the port-holes, perfectly illuminating the interior so that, when he passed into the inner cabin, the gold was clearly visible.

The bars of gold lay in a jumbled mass in the angle of the cabin roof. Presumably when the launch had tilted the boxes must have been smashed open against the bulkheads. He picked up one of the bars and found it comparatively light to handle. It retarded his rate of progress to the surface a little but he kicked strongly and his rubber flippers did the trick. He came out into the sunlight and Mason leaned over and took the bar from him. Hagen pulled himself over the rail and they all gathered round. 'It doesn't look like much,' Rose said in a disappointed tone.

Hagen laughed and pulled his heavy sheath knife from his belt and scraped the dull metal surface of the block. The gold showed through, suddenly glinting in the sunlight, and

O'Hara whistled. They examined the bar in silence for a moment. Mason was the first to speak. 'How much do you think it's worth?'

Hagen weighed the bar in his hands for a moment. 'Hard to be accurate,' he answered. 'I'd say this bar weighs about five pounds. Should be worth in the region of two thousand five hundred dollars.'

Mason's eyes gleamed momentarily and then his expression changed. 'That means there must be a hell of a lot of bars to bring up.'

'I was wondering when you'd realize that,' Hagen said. 'About a hundred, I'd say.'

Rose had been listening quietly and now she interrupted. 'I think there were five boxes originally, Mark.'

He nodded. 'What I'll try to do is repack the bars and secure the boxes in a cocoon of rope. That way they should hold long enough to be hauled to the surface.'

'It's going to take a long while, lad,' O'Hara told him.

'It would take a damned sight longer to bring the stuff up a bar at a time,' Hagen said with a shrug.

The necessary precautions were quickly made. O'Hara and Mason swung the spar from which the block and tackle were suspended out over the side and lowered the heavy hook and cable down into the water. When Hagen dived for the second time he carried a spare coil of rope with him. He followed the cable down to the bottom of the lagoon, and picking up the hook, dragged it behind him when he entered the launch.

The task was easier than he had expected. Three of the boxes seemed to be in quite good condition and only their lids had been shattered when they had smashed into the bulkheads. He carefully packed twenty bars of the gold into one of the good boxes and then bound it securely with rope. He fastened the hook into position and then jerked on the cable giving the prearranged signal. O'Hara and Mason began to heave and the box lifted a little and jerked across the cabin. Hagen followed, helping it over the rough spots and through the doors and, finally, out on to the deck. The rest was easy. He followed it up to the surface and clambered on board as

O'Hara and Mason swung it in over the deck. Mason was jubilant. 'Thirty-five minutes,' he said. 'Pretty good going.'

As they uncoiled the rope from around the box Hagen rested. 'It may not be so easy with some of the others,' he said. 'This was probably the best of the boxes.' As he spoke, O'Hara uncoiled the last twist of rope and the box gently burst open at one side. 'See what I mean?' Hagen said.

He dived again and repeated the operation with the other two good boxes. He worked steadily, taking his time, and stayed in the water when the second box was raised. It was about eleven-thirty when the third box was successfully on deck and he decided to take a break. He was sitting on deck having a smoke and a cup of coffee when Chang came out of the reeds in a large and roomy canoe. O'Hara threw him a line and he hopped over the rail and stood before them bowing and smiling hugely. He was wearing a spotless white shirt and blue silk pantaloons. Around his brow was a headband made by a brilliant silk scarf of many colours.

'Greetings, lord,' he said to Hagen. 'I bring the thanks of my family.'

Hagen gave him a cigarette and the fisherman squatted down on the deck and puffed away with every evidence of enjoyment. 'What of your brother?' Hagen asked him. 'Have you buried him yet?'

Chang nodded and explained that the funeral had taken place that morning. It had been an occasion for much rejoicing, not only by his family, but by the entire village. There was to be a celebration that evening and they were all invited. Hagen refused, showing the proper amount of reluctance. 'We have much work yet to finish,' he said, 'and at evening we must move back to the sea.' Chang looked very disappointed and Hagen added, 'Have your people noticed any strangers in the marshes or any of the Government men who wear the Red Star?'

Chang shook his head. 'You are the only outsiders here, lord. Our young men fish in every part of the marshes. We would know at once if strangers appeared.'

Hagen translated for the benefit of Mason

201

and O'Hara, and Mason grinned. 'Things are looking up,' he said. 'We'll be waiting for that boat right on schedule in the morning.'

Hagen nodded and Chang scrambled to his feet and prepared to leave. 'Is there anything I can do for you, lord?' he asked.

Before Hagen could reply Rose interrupted him and spoke directly to the fishermen. 'Have you fish or fresh fruit?'

He nodded. 'I will return in two hours.'

Rose caught his arm as he prepared to climb over the rail, and turned to Hagen. 'I'm going to go with him, Mark,' she said.

Hagen was astounded. 'Don't be crazy,' he said. 'You can't go off on your own in this place.'

'Why not?' Rose demanded. 'We're the only intruders, as Chang just told you. I'll be safe enough in the marshes with him and there's nothing I can do here except stand and watch. Steve and O'Hara won't let me lift the bars – they say they're too heavy.'

Mason laughed. 'Let her go if she wants to. There's nobody around in these marshes that Chang and his pals don't know about. She'll be back in a couple of hours.'

Hagen still felt reluctant but she brushed any further argument aside by scrambling over the rail and dropping down into the canoe. Chang seated himself in the stern and as they moved away she turned and waved at Hagen. 'Don't worry,' she called. 'See you soon.'

For a brief moment Hagen stood watching and as they disappeared into the reeds Mason said, 'Too late to stop her now.' Hagen nodded and as he tightened the straps of the aqua-lung a vague uneasiness stirred within him.

He worked hard for the next hour. The two remaining boxes were almost in pieces and it took patience and concentrated effort to rope them successfully together. The first box was hauled to the surface without incident. As he ventured into the cabin for the last time and hooked the remaining box to the cable he was conscious of a feeling of distinct relief. It had gone more smoothly than he would have dared to hope. He lifted the box through the entrance and it began a slow and jerky ascent through the water. For a moment he watched it with satisfaction and then he started to follow it. Suddenly one side of the box bulged, and five or six bars squeezed through the strained coils of rope and cascaded downwards to the bottom of the lagoon.

The whole thing happened in a second and the bars seemed to glide down in slow motion. Hagen poised in mid-water gazing at them in stupefaction until one of them grazed his shoulder. The pain of the heavy blow galvanized him into life again and he twisted out of the path of the other bars. He drifted up to the surface and Mason reached down and hauled him over the rail. Hagen jerked away with his breathing-tube and swore violently. 'What luck!' he said.

Mason handed him a lighted cigarette. 'It could have been worse,' he said. 'You'll have to bring up the odd bars singly.'

Hagen laughed sharply. 'Hell, you're right,' he said. 'We can't grumble. Everything's gone marvellously until now.' He slumped down on the engine-room hatch and inhaled the cigarette smoke with pleasure.

O'Hara was busily engaged in freeing the box from its cocoon of rope and Hagen saw that much of the gold had already disappeared from the deck. The old man kept stopping and listening and suddenly he spat into the lagoon and stood up. 'I don't like it,' he said.

Mason turned in surprise. 'What's up with you?' he said.

'It's the birds,' the old man replied. 'Ever since we've been in this stinking plague-spot they've done nothing but make a row. Now there isn't a sound from any of them.'

For a moment they all listened and Hagen was conscious of a cold finger of fear that moved in his stomach. 'He's right,' Mason said abruptly. 'There isn't a sound from the wildfowl.'

Hagen got to his feet. Something was wrong. Something was very damned wrong. There was a sudden flurry of movement and a great cloud of birds lifted skywards from the reeds. 'It stinks,' he said. 'There's something going on.' He moved to the rail and adjusted his diving equipment.

'What are you going to do?' Mason said.

'I'll bring these bars up as fast as I can,' Hagen told him. 'After that we've got some fast thinking to do.'

He worked quickly, with a minimum of effort. There were six bars and he brought them up from the bottom of the lagoon, one at a time. The sixth had fallen a few feet away from the others and when he returned for it he had to search in a small cloud of sand, raised by his feet each time he had kicked towards the surface. He found the bar at last and started to rise, and it was then that he saw the keel of the canoe, moving through the water towards *Hurrier*.

His first thought was that Rose had returned sooner than she had expected and relief flooded through him. He surfaced a few feet away from the canoe and started to submerge almost in the same moment. Its occupants were two Chinese in drab and dirty uniforms. In their caps was the Red Star of the Army of the People's Republic. One of the soldiers was standing up in the prow, menacing Mason and O'Hara with a machine-pistol. As Hagen submerged the man swung his weapon in an arc and fired a long burst. Hagen descended again and watched the stream of bullets enter the water and then lose their velocity and sink slowly downwards, harmless pieces of lead. He released his grip on the remaining gold bar and kicked strongly towards the keel of the canoe. The rubber flippers propelled him upwards with considerable force. As his head bumped gently into the canoe, he gripped the edge with both hands and pulled the frail craft completely over.

One of the soldiers sprawled against him, his legs thrashing the water, and Hagen grabbed him by the belt and towed him down into the deep water. He wrapped his legs around the rail of the launch and clamped a forearm round the man's throat. It wasn't pretty watching him die. He struggled violently, his limbs moving sluggishly, and there was a nightmarish edge of horror to the whole thing. Suddenly a clawing hand reached back and wrenched the breathing-tube from

Hagen's mouth. Hagen compressed his lips and tightened his grip. Blood began to seep from the man's nostrils in two clouds and a moment later he swung loosely against Hagen's arm. Hagen unlocked his fingers and let go. The body bounced away, spun round twice, and settled on to the floor of the lagoon.

There was a roaring in his ears and his temples pounded. He kicked out sharply for the surface and then above him and slightly to one side he saw a tremendous disturbance. It was Mason and the other soldier, locked together, and from the looks of it Mason was not having things all his own way. It was neither the time nor the place for chivalry. He swam towards them, jerking the heavy knife from the sheath at his belt as he approached. He pushed the knife blindly into the soldier's back, using both hands, and kicked for the surface.

He bumped against the side of *Hurrier*, choking and gasping for breath. A second later Mason surfaced a few feet away. O'Hara pulled them over the rail, one after the other, and they lay on the deck, coughing violently. After a while Hagen sat up and began to check the aqua-lung and his breathing-tube. 'What are you going to do?' Mason demanded.

Hagen scrambled wearily to his feet. 'Going after that last bar,' he said. 'I think I can just make it.'

'You're mad!' O'Hara screamed. 'That bloody gold's sent you off your head.'

Hagen spat and coughed a little. 'I'm not leaving two and a half thousand down there for the sake of a few minutes' work and a couple of stiffs,' he said and lowered himself over the rail.

As he sank slowly down through the water he felt utterly weary and a little light-headed. If a thing's worth doing at all it's worth doing right, he thought, and he twisted his body and hung suspended over the remaining bar. As his hands fastened over it he suddenly realized the difference between himself and the other two. There was a limit to what they would do – even for money. But not yours truly, he thought sleepily, as he drifted up towards the surface, away from the body that bounced on the sands of the lagoon and the other that slowly descended in a cloud of blood. Mason reached down and took the bar from him. His face was strained and there was something in his eyes, an expression that Hagen couldn't quite analyse. 'You're a fool, Hagen,' the big man said as he hauled him on to the deck. 'But I'll say this for you. You've got more cold-blooded guts than any man I've ever met.'

'Save the compliments,' Hagen gasped. For a moment he stood swaying against the wheel-house and then he said: 'For Christ's sake help me to get this gear off. We've got to get moving.'

Mason and O'Hara stripped the diving equipment from him and he went below and dressed quickly. His head was splitting and he lit a cigarette with shaking fingers and spat it out in disgust at the taste of it. Mason flopped down on the opposite bunk and O'Hara stood in the doorway. 'What are we going to do, lad?' the old man said.

Hagen took out one of the carbines and loaded it. 'We're going to look for her,' he said, and as the words issued from his lips another voice was saying silently: 'Don't be a fool. Get out of it with the gold while you can, before the whole thing blows up in your face.'

Mason laughed flatly. 'Don't be a bloody fool,' he said. 'We don't even know where the village is.' He straightened up and ran a hand through his damp hair. 'All we can do is sit tight and wait.'

'But they must be here!' Hagen exploded. 'Kossoff and the whole bloody bunch. Chang was wrong. Somehow they've fooled us.'

Mason lifted a hand. 'So Kossoff pulled a fast one. So Chang and his pals were wrong for once. Okay! But Rose is safer with that fisherman than she is with us or I miss my guess. Those guys will never find him unless he wants them to.' Hagen started to speak and Mason said flatly, 'We've got to sit tight and wait.' Hagen suddenly crumpled up inside. He dropped the carbine on the table and threw himself down on his bunk with his face to the wall. A sense of utter frustration filled him, and as the pounding in his brain increased he turned and buried his head in the pillow.

Mercifully his mind had stood enough and he drifted into a state of semi-consciousness. It was a state that lay half-way between waking and sleeping and he hung there, suspended, as though he were back again in the waters of the lagoon, poised over the launch, and his mind became a blank and he thought of nothing.

It was as if he had awakened from a deep and refreshing sleep. For a moment he lay quietly on the bunk, not stirring. He felt relaxed and in command of himself again and his mind was razor sharp. From the other bunk came the sound of Mason's deep, even breathing and of O'Hara there was no sign. A hot, brooding quiet hung over everything and yet Hagen knew that something had disturbed him. He slipped from the bunk and awakened Mason quietly, clamping a hand over his mouth. He picked up the carbine from the table and went out on deck, Mason at his heels.

O'Hara lay snoring softly in the sun, his back against the wheelhouse. Mason wakened him gently and placed a finger over his lips.

The old man's eyes widened and moved slowly to Hagen and then towards the reeds. There was a sound of splashing and they waited tensely, and then a canoe came through the reeds and in the bow was huddled a hunched-up figure.

It was Chang, and as he came alongside they saw that his clothing was muddied and torn and there was blood on his face. A flap of flesh hung from one cheek and flies gorged themselves on the congealing blood. They pulled him over the rail and lowered him gently down on the deck and O'Hara brought one of the bottles of rum and poured some down his throat. Chang coughed violently and a little life returned to his eyes. He had obviously received a terrible beating and as Hagen examined him, fear moved in him. Finally the fisherman managed to speak and told them his story in short, incoherent sentences. Hagen translated for the others, a sentence at a time.

They had arrived at the village without incident. Chang had noticed the silence of the villagers, who appeared to be working at their nets. As they landed, a party of soldiers had rushed from the shelter of the huts from where they had silently threatened the villagers. Chang had attempted to put up a defence but had been clubbed into the ground with rifle butts. When he regained consciousness he was lying in one of the huts. There was no guard on the door and he'd managed to crawl away to a place where he knew he would find an old canoe.

After he had finished talking there was silence and Mason cursed and said, 'What do you think?'

Hagen shook his head slowly. 'I don't know. There's no proof that it's Kossoff – might just be a sudden invasion by an army patrol.' He shivered suddenly. 'I hope to God it is Kossoff. She'll be better off in his hands than the soldiers'!'

Mason laughed bitterly. 'Just when everything looked so nice.' He stood up. 'Well, when do we put our necks under the sword?'

Hagen smiled tightly. 'The sooner the better. He mightn't expect us to move so fast. Get a Thompson and a few grenades.' As

Mason went into the cabin Hagen turned to O'Hara and said: 'I'll leave you here. If we aren't back by dark we shan't be coming. You'll have to try to reach the sea on your own.'

The old man nodded heavily and Mason appeared with the sub-machine-guns. He had several grenades clipped to his belt. Hagen dropped down into the canoe and Mason followed him, seating himself in the stern. Chang scrambled into the prow and he and Mason did the paddling. O'Hara didn't bother to say goodbye as they moved away from the boat and plunged into the reeds and Hagen thought: He doesn't expect to see us again. We're dead already to him. He shivered and gripped the carbine fiercely.

They passed through the reeds and into the waterway and they were at once in another world, away from the quiet of the secret lagoon, back amongst the stench and the mosquitoes. As sweat began to pour down his face Hagen glared around him at the marsh and hated it as he had never done before.

After about half an hour of hard paddling Chang turned his head and told him that the village was now only a few hundred yards away. They entered a long strip of open water, the surface of which was completely covered with lily pads and thick green scum. They were about half-way across the water, the prow of the canoe cutting through the lilies, when an automatic weapon opened up from the shelter of the reeds in front of them. Chang gave a terrible scream and fell backwards against Hagen, his chest and stomach neatly sieved.

Hagen lifted his carbine and sprayed the reeds and from the corner of his eye he was aware of Mason frantically trying to pull the sling of the Tommy-gun over his head. Bullets lifted the water into Hagen's face and he emptied the magazine into the reeds. As he hurriedly fitted another clip, Mason cried out sharply and stood up, his hand over his face, blood pouring through the fingers. For a moment he swayed and then overbalanced into the water and the canoe went with him.

The carbine slipped from Hagen's grasp and

he came to the surface gasping for air and half-choked by the foul, evil-smelling water. He saw Mason's face, pale and blood-spattered, and struck out towards him, but he had already disappeared beneath the surface before Hagen could reach the spot.

At that moment a canoe bumped into his back. He lifted his head and caught a confused glimpse of several Chinese faces and, most clearly, a rifle that was raised and lowered very rapidly towards him, and then the whole world rocked in a black explosion laced with coloured lights.

10

He lay with his cheek pillowed on the earth
and regarded the boots through half-open
eyes. They were battered and filthy and
surmounted by greasy, khaki puttees. After a
while one of them swung forward and dug
into his ribs. He groaned suddenly as pain
knifed into him and his vision blurred slightly.
He lay in the dirt, fighting for breath, and
watched the boots walk across the floor, kick
open a door, and disappear. After a minute
he felt a little better and dragged himself up
into a sitting position.

He was in one corner of a crude hut with
clay-daubed walls and an earthen floor. The
stench was indescribable, and when his eyes

became accustomed to the gloom, he saw that in another corner was a pile of human dung and nearby lay two men. There was a crack in the wall behind him and he pulled himself painfully to his feet and examined his condition.

One side of his skull was badly swollen, the hair matted and sticky with congealed blood. His groping hand scattered a cloud of flies and a shudder ran through him. He gently flexed his muscles and swung his arms, stifling a cry as pain swept through him from the bruise left by that boot in the ribs. He crossed the floor to examine his fellow-prisoners. Nausea flooded through him and he swayed and groped at the wall, but after a moment his senses returned and he knelt down to examine the two men.

They were two of the villagers, both dead. From the looks of it, they had been terribly beaten and thrown into the hut without medical attention of any kind. A cloud of flies lifted from one of the bodies and Hagen turned his head away and vomited. He staggered to his feet and lurched over to the other side of the hut and sat down. The sanitary conditions were an indication not only of the standards of the Chinese soldiery, but also of their stupidity. He reflected that a few short hours of the stifling heat would do unbelievable things to the corpses. A disease could spring up that would sweep through the village. A fly alighted on his face and he brushed it away impatiently and scrambled to his feet.

The door had been left half open. The wearer of the boots must have concluded that Hagen's condition was worse than it actually was and that he would be in no condition to move for some time. Hagen leaned in the doorway, breathing the comparatively pure air and blinking in the strong sunlight. The village lay sleeping in the afternoon heat. Perhaps thirty huts huddled together on an island surrounded by marsh. A shabby, forty-foot motor launch was tied up alongside a rough wooden jetty that stretched out into the water. There was no sign of activity on its deck and from the mast the flag of Red China drooped listlessly in the afternoon heat.

The silence was shattered by a sudden scream and a young Chinese girl ran from a nearby hut. She was completely naked. Immediately behind came two soldiers and one of them caught her by the wrist and whirled her round and hit her in the face. The girl crumpled to the ground and the two grinning solders carried her between them back to the hut.

Hagen had stepped back into the gloom of the hut as he watched. He felt sick again. For a terrible moment he had imagined that the girl was Rose and he shuddered as it came to him that such a scene had perhaps already been enacted. For a moment he hesitated and then he straightened his shoulders and stepped out into the sunlight. He paused, looking about him, wondering what to do, and then he heard sharp, excited Chinese voices and three soldiers ran towards him, rifles at the ready.

Bayonets pricked into his unwilling flesh, urging him forward towards a larger and better-made hut, obviously the home of the local headman. He hesitated at the bottom of the half-dozen steps that led up to the small verandah and a boot thudded into him driving him forward. He hesitated again in the doorway, peering into the cool darkness of the hut, and a hand pushed flatly into the small of his back.

Hagen winced as pain tugged at his kidneys and in a sudden upsurge of rage he kicked backwards, his heel connecting satisfactorily with a knee-cap. The Chinese soldier behind him screamed and Hagen twisted to avoid the rifle, and, pulling the man forward, slammed his head twice against the wall. For a moment he stared into the face of death as the bayonets of the other two flickered towards him and then a voice shouted a command in Cantonese. The two soldiers immediately lowered their weapons, and picking up the body of their fallen comrade, dragged it outside. A voice said in English: 'Come in, Captain Hagen. What a violent man you are.' It was Kossoff.

Hagen moved forward and found him sitting in a sort of basket chair at a rude table. There was a chair opposite him and Hagen sat down and helped himself to the gin that stood on the table, drinking from the bottle. He toasted Kossoff silently and drank again. As the liquor flooded through him he felt better. He leaned back in the chair and said: 'All the comforts of home, eh? You boys certainly have it rough working for the proletariat. By the way, you haven't got a cigarette have you? My last packet got slightly damp.'

The Russian produced a packet of American cigarettes from his pocket and threw them across the table with a quick flip of the fingers. 'You see, my dear Captain, I can supply all your requirements.'

Hagen extracted a cigarette and leaned across for the proffered light. 'What's the matter with your own brands?' he said, indicating the packet of cigarettes.

Kossoff smiled pleasantly. 'But Virginia cigarettes are extremely good. When our time comes we shall undoubtedly take them all for home consumption.'

Hagen smiled, unable to resist baiting the man. 'Careful, Comrade. In Moscow they would call that treason.'

Kossoff smiled and adjusted a cigarette in his elegant holder. 'But we are not in Moscow now, my dear Captain. Here I am in control. I must confess to having no great liking for the locale but I am sure that with your co-operation we can all adjourn speedily to more pleasant surroundings.'

Hagen was interested. There was still a suggestion that a deal could be made. Suddenly he frowned. But why? he thought. He's got all the good cards. I haven't got a hope and he knows it. He smiled at the Russian through smoke and said, 'So there's still a chance for me?'

Kossoff nodded and smiled benignly. 'And for Miss Graham.' He leaned forward and said confidentially: 'I must confess that one of the more charming aspects of this whole business has been making her acquaintance. Such an exquisite bloom to find in this pest-hole.'

Hagen controlled himself with difficulty and schooled a smile to his face. 'Yes, she's quite a girl.'

The Russian nodded. 'Unfortunately, rather

stubborn.' As Hagen leaned forward he raised a hand. 'Oh, don't alarm yourself, Captain. She is quite unharmed. I have no intention of hurting her – yet.'

For some time there was silence and Hagen moved uneasily in the rough chair. What was Kossoff playing at? Why the cat-and-mouse game? He stubbed his cigarette carefully and said: 'What about my friend? Did your boys bring him in?'

Kossoff gently shook his head. 'They didn't even look for the body. They considered that a bullet in the head was all they could be expected to do for him.' He sighed despairingly. 'They are just savages, you know – ignorant savages. Children really.'

Hagen grimaced and said bitterly, 'Yes – children.'

The Russian tapped the table with one elegant hand and said reflectively, 'It's a very great pity.'

His voice sighed out of the quiet and Hagen listened to him in a curiously detached sort of way and thought of other things at the same time. 'What is?'

'The fact that we are on opposite sides.' He chuckled and continued: 'After all, Captain Hagen, I am not a political idealist; I am not a fanatic. I am a man who likes the good things of life and I have always adjusted myself to the prevailing circumstances. In that way I have survived – comfortably. You might say that I am a sort of opportunist. I thought that we had at least that much in common but you have disappointed me, my friend. I cannot understand your attitude to this affair.' There was a curious note of regret in his voice.

Hagen's brain worked overtime, creating and rejecting plans to meet the situation. He only replied to keep the conversation going: 'You can't trust anybody these days, Kossoff. You should know that more than anyone.'

Steps moved behind him and a voice spoke in clipped English. 'This is really a waste of time, Comrade. We are getting nowhere.'

Hagen turned his head. Behind him stood a small, balding Chinese officer in wrinkled uniform. The man wiped sweat from his pock-marked, evil face, and Kossoff said: 'Allow me to introduce Captain Tsen. He has been good enough to co-operate with me in this business.'

Hagen turned back to Kossoff and said: 'He's quite right, of course. We are getting nowhere.'

Kossoff smiled and blew smoke up to the ceiling in a long, delicate plume. 'Somewhere in those damned reeds is your boat. Presumably you've got the gold. The time has come for us to make terms.' His smile widened and he looked directly at Hagen. 'Your attitude to this whole affair has always puzzled me, as I said before, but now I have a theory. Let us experiment.' He raised his voice and shouted in Cantonese, 'Send in the lady.'

Hagen reached for the gin bottle and took another pull and then a door opened in the darkness at the rear of the room. When he lowered his eyes he saw Rose step slowly forward. For a moment she hesitated and then her eyes widened in recognition and she stumbled forward and fell into his arms as he rose to meet her. 'It's all right, angel,' he said, and patted her head awkwardly. 'It's going to be fine.'

Kossoff laughed softly and said: 'But who would have thought it? The young lovers.'

Hagen looked at him over her shoulder and said, 'Okay, what happens now?'

Tsen moved forward quickly and wrenched the girl away from him. He slapped Hagen back-handed across the face. 'You will lead us to your boat!' he screamed.

Hagen took a pace forward and out of the corner of his eye saw the automatic appear in Kossoff's hand. 'Why should I?' he said. 'You'll kill us anyway.' Captain Tsen lifted his foot up smartly into Hagen's groin.

As he writhed on the floor he was dimly aware of Kossoff's voice snarling viciously at the captain. 'You fool!' he screamed. 'We need him in one piece. That isn't the way to handle this man. If you want your share you'd better leave things to me.'

And then it all came clear to Hagen so that even through the agony that gripped his loins with fire, he managed to smile, mirthlessly, through clenched teeth. After a few

229

moments he hauled himself up and stood leaning on the table. He began to laugh. It was all so plain now. The reason for the lack of naval forces to prevent his entry into the marshes. The one shabby motor launch, the handful of soldiers. He laughed again and said to Kossoff: 'You bloody twister. I might have known. You want the gold for yourself.'

Rose moved to his side and gently eased him back into the chair and Kossoff laughed pleasantly. 'But of course. Has it taken you so long to discover that? After all, it is one desire that we have in common.'

There was a short, electric silence and Rose said in a low, angry voice, 'That's a lie.'

Kossoff smiled gently. 'Ask him. Surely you were not so naïve as to believe that everything he did was for love.'

She turned and looked straight into Hagen's eyes. There was a puzzled frown on her forehead. 'Tell him it isn't true, Mark.'

For a moment he wanted to lie. It would have been easy to refute the charge and she would have believed him because she wanted to believe, but suddenly he felt sick. Sick of the whole damned thing. He dropped his eyes and reached blindly for another cigarette from Kossoff's packet. 'No, he's right; angel,' he said. 'The man's one hundred per cent correct.'

She turned away quickly. For a moment he waited, expecting a blow, but when he raised his eyes he saw that she was gazing out of the window with a strange expression on her face. She said slowly, 'You won't get any help from us – from either of us.' She moved her head and looked directly into Hagen's eyes.

For a moment he held her gaze and then he shivered and a queer fatalism ran through him. He stood up. 'She's right, Kossoff,' he said. 'You can scour the marshes from now till Domesday.'

Kossoff bowed suddenly from the waist. 'I salute you, my dear,' he said to Rose. 'You are a most remarkable young woman.' He made a gesture to Tsen who nodded and went out quickly through the front door.

Hagen suddenly felt weary and in a funny

way he was happy. He grinned tiredly. From the beginning he had known deep inside him that the girl would never agree to use the gold for a wrong purpose. For the first time he realized what it must have meant to her. Her father had died for it. It had been placed in his charge as a trust and the trust had passed on to her. Hagen smiled briefly. To think that in this world he should have found someone who still lived by a code. Honour! It had been a long time since he had forced himself to face the implications of that word. From outside came a shouted command and Kossoff said: 'Please come out on to the verandah. There is something I would like you to watch.'

They moved outside and stood at the top of the steps, and twenty or thirty yards away there were four soldiers standing to attention. On the ground a fisherman, one of the villagers, was pegged-out, face downwards, his legs wrenched cruelly apart. The man was quite naked. A few paces to the rear of him Captain Tsen was standing. In one hand he carried a three-foot bamboo pole, the end sharpened and pointed like a needle. Kossoff nodded and Tsen got down on his knees beside the unfortunate fisherman.

Rose turned away at once. She tried to rush into the hut but Kossoff barred the way. She turned to Hagen and buried her head against his shoulder. The screams were unbelievable. For a few moments Hagen gazed in fascinated horror and then he looked at Kossoff. The Russian was observing the scene with a detached interest. There was not the slightest trace of sadism in his face. He snapped a command and two soldiers moved forward and stood at the bottom of the steps. For a moment Hagen went cold and then Kossoff said, 'Follow me, please.'

They crossed the open space and moved back towards the prison but Hagen said, 'Now what?'

They paused outside the hut and the Russian gazed up at him seriously. 'You've got half an hour,' he said. 'The girl can stay with you. The attractions inside may help her to make up her mind.' He turned and gestured towards the little group in front of the headman's hut. 'I don't need to threaten. If, when I come for you in half an hour, you are not prepared to lead us to your boat, then one of you will have to be next.' A strange expression was in his eyes as he added: 'Believe me, Hagen. I do not want to do it. Don't make me.' He walked away and the two soldiers pushed Hagen and the girl into the hut and closed the door.

Hagen led her into the corner that was farthest away from the two bodies and held her very close as her whole body shook with sobs. After a while she seemed a little better but when she spoke there was still horror in her voice. 'That was unbelievable,' she said. 'It was like something out of a horrible dream.'

He pulled her down into the corner. 'Don't worry,' he said. 'It won't happen to you, I'll see to that.'

'You're going to tell him?' Her voice was very quiet.

He nodded. 'He doesn't make idle threats. He'll carry out his promise.'

She was silent for a while and finally said:

'Mark, why did you deceive me? I trusted you. I really did.'

He shrugged. 'Does it matter now? I needed the money. It was an escape.' He laughed shortly. 'Maybe you won't believe me but you were going to get a fair share. I wasn't going to leave you on the beach.'

She nodded and said sadly: 'Yes, I believe you. I believe you.' Suddenly she cried out sharply and hammered a clenched fist into his shoulder. 'Oh, that damned gold. Why does it change people so? Why does it have to be so important?'

He put an arm around her shoulders. 'It doesn't change people, angel. Just shows them in their true colours.'

She leaned against him and closed her eyes and Hagen stared blindly into space and wondered how he could have been such a fool. I should have listened to Clara, he thought, and a tiny smile tugged at his mouth because he knew that it wasn't so much anger or fear that was annoying him. It was the fact that she knew him for what he was and he admitted to himself that it was important to him to have her good opinion. From somewhere in the region of his back there came a tiny, persistent scraping sound.

For a few moments he did not move and then he quickly placed his mouth to the girl's ear. 'Don't make a sound,' he breathed. He turned and crouched beside the wall and listened and then a tiny hole appeared and a knife blade was inserted and suddenly a large piece of the dried mud flaked away. Hagen peered out into the pale, haggard face of Mason.

For a moment they stared at each other and then Mason whispered, 'Surprise, surprise!' There was a bloodstained piece of rag tied round his head and deep pain in his eyes. 'Bullet only creased me,' he said. 'I was watching that little show of Kossoff's from the reeds. Saw them bring you to this hut.'

Hagen had never been so glad to see anyone in his life before. 'The two monkeys on the door won't bother us for a while,' he said. 'Have you any arms?'

Mason passed the sub-machine-gun through. 'Slightly damp but it should still do the job and I've still got two grenades. Lost the others in the water.' Rose pushed her face against the hole and he grinned and said, 'Hello, baby. Let's have you out of there.'

He and Mason started to pull away large pieces of the mud and wattle wall with their hands. In a few moments the hole was large enough for them to pass through. Rose crawled out and he followed her. They crouched by the side of the hut and Mason motioned them to silence. There was no sound except for the low murmuring of the two guards in front of the hut. Mason pointed to a bamboo thicket that stood about twenty yards away and they moved towards it quickly, Hagen bringing up the rear with the sub-machine-gun. They were still some yards from shelter when a shout came from behind them. Hagen turned quickly and loosed a burst off as a reflex action. One of the guards was half-way through the hole in the wall of the hut. He screamed as the bullets pushed him back through the hole and then the other one rushed round from the front of the hut shouting for help at the top of his voice.

As he raised his rifle Hagen fired another burst that lifted the man backwards and spun him round. He turned and plunged into the bamboos after Mason and Rose.

As they stumbled through the thicket, arms raised to ward off the flailing bamboos, Hagen gasped, 'What do we do now?'

Mason answered briefly over his shoulder. 'I managed to refloat our canoe after they left me for dead. I've left her hidden in the reeds. We'll have to do some wading though.'

From then on all talk died. In the distance they could hear the sounds of pursuit and Hagen knew that he'd had his last chance with Kossoff. There would be no charity next time. Rose stumbled once and he caught her but she shook off his helping hand and staggered on. Suddenly they were through the bamboos and out in the open. They began to run over a wide expanse of open ground covered with coarse marsh-grass and then the ground became soft and they sank ankle deep into the waterlogged soil. As they progressed the going became tougher. They had not far to go now. The shelter of the reeds lay only forty or fifty yards ahead and still their pursuers had not come out into the open.

The evil, scum-covered waters of the marsh reached out to greet them and suddenly they were waist deep. 'We're going to do it,' Hagen thought. 'We're going to do it.' At that moment Rose stumbled and fell and as Mason turned to lift her there was a sudden shout of triumph. A bullet landed in the water beside them and Hagen turned and fired quickly at the group of soldiers who had appeared from the bamboos. Two of them cried out and fell down and the others ran back into the shelter of the thicket.

Hagan turned and followed Mason and Rose and the water lifted to his armpits and then the reeds were all around him and he knew that for the moment they were safe.

11

As they plunged deeper into the reeds the level of the water dropped until it was only waist deep. Progress was still made difficult by the thick, glutinous slime which the water covered and which was in some places knee deep. From behind came the calls of their pursuers and Hagen tightened his grip on his weapon. Whatever happened he was resolved that they would not fall into Kossoff's hands again.

Suddenly the water deepened and Rose stumbled and disappeared under the surface. They hauled her upright and she pushed dark tendrils of hair away from her eyes. 'Are you all right?' Hagen asked.

'I'm fine! Really I am. Let's keep moving.'

They started to move forward again and now the reeds began to thin a little and the cover was less adequate. After a while Mason held up his hand and stopped. He looked about him searchingly and there was an expression of doubt on his face. 'Where the hell did you leave the canoe?' Hagen demanded fiercely.

There was an edge of panic in Mason's voice. 'I'm not sure. I thought I'd find it easily but it wasn't as far away from the village as this.'

Hagen cursed and raised an arm to wipe the sweat from his face. What luck. What stinking, God-awful luck. From quite nearby there came a crashing sound as bodies forced their way through the reeds. 'Let's get out of here,' Mason hissed. 'Those bastards are getting too close for comfort.'

They plunged on, getting deeper and deeper into the marsh, and from behind them came the sound of relentless pursuit. They all fell several times, for the swampy water was treacherous and had a way of changing in depth without warning. Once Hagen stepped into a deep hole and the water completely covered his head. He struggled back to a comparatively safe footing, cursing and spitting, but always the sounds of hunters grew nearer and nearer. They emerged unexpectedly into a broad expanse of shallow water. For a moment Mason hesitated and Hagen cried savagely, 'Keep going, for God's sake, man.' He pushed a hand in Mason's back that almost sent the big man flat on his face and they started across towards the shelter of the reeds that lay fifty or sixty yards away. They had almost covered the distance when the shooting began.

Bullets churned the water beside them and Hagen grabbed Rose by the arm and forced her forward into the shelter of the reeds. They turned and looked back. Four soldiers, rifles at the ready, plunged knee-deep through the water, shrill cries of triumph on their lips. Mason reached for the grenades he had clipped to his belt and swore violently. 'Only one left. I must have lost the other on the way.'

'Make sure it does the job,' Hagen told him. 'We can't afford mistakes.'

Everything seemed to focus on the small group of men, water boiling around their knees as they charged forward, their voices somehow unreal and fragile in the stifling heat of that place. They seemed to be suddenly too near for safety and Hagen raised the sub-machine-gun and took careful aim and then the grenade drifted lazily through the air in a long curve and settled amongst them. For a single breathless second there was the silence of shock and then one of the men screamed a warning. As they turned to scatter water erupted in their midst in a brilliant flash that reached out and enfolded them. For a little while the sky rained debris and then great clouds of marsh fowl lifted into the sky in waves, their terrified crying drowning the screams of the dying men.

Rose shuddered and turned a horrified face to Hagen. 'Is there no end to this?' she said. 'Is there only death and destruction?'

There was a glazed look in her eyes and Hagen knew that she had been pushed too far. He pulled her on to her feet roughly. 'Let's keep moving,' he said. 'Keep bearing east. That's roughly where we want to be.'

There was no hope of getting back to the launch without a canoe. There was no hope and yet he still kept resolutely on, pushing the weary girl before him. Mason fell several times. The last time he seemed to have difficulty regaining his feet and when Hagen stumbled forward to help him he saw that fresh blood was seeping from underneath the crude bandage. 'Are you all right?' he said.

Mason nodded and smiled tightly. 'I'll be fine. Lost a lot of blood, that's all. Made me a bit light-headed.' He turned and moved forward without resting.

And then they heard the sound of an engine. They halted, crouching low down in the water, and Hagen said, 'They've got the launch out.' He made a sudden decision. 'We'll follow the sound of it.'

'You're crazy,' Mason croaked. 'You want to walk right into Kossoff's hands?'

Hagen explained impatiently. 'Don't you see? The launch must be in deep water. If we can once find that main channel I think I can find the way back to *Hurrier*.'

'How we going to get there – swim?' Mason demanded.

Hagen didn't answer and they moved forward again. The water began to deepen appreciately. The engine of the launch sounded quite near now and then the water was up to their armpits and Hagen held the sub-machine-gun high above his head. The reeds parted before them and he found himself on the edge of a strip of open water. The surface of the water was covered thickly with lily pads and the place looked vaguely familiar. Mason grinned and there was new hope in his voice. 'This is the place where we were ambushed.'

Hagen nodded. 'You're right.'

'Think you could find the way back from here?' Mason said.

'I think so.' Rose lurched wearily against him and Hagen slipped an arm about her shoulders. At that moment the launch's engines grew louder. 'Move back,' Hagen said sharply and they melted into the shelter of the reeds.

The launch moved slowly back in the direction of the village, and as they ducked even lower into the water, its bow wave passed over them. Through the reeds Hagen saw Kossoff standing in the prow. He looked very angry. The launch disappeared and the sound grew fainter and Mason said, 'Do you think they're giving up?'

'Not him,' Hagen said. 'Only when he's dead.'

Rose coughed and said in a weak voice, 'I'm sorry, Mark, but I can't take much more of this.'

He held her tightly in his left arm and wondered what the hell they were going to do and then, through the heat of the evening, there sounded a splash of paddles and the bird-like chatter of Chinese voices. He peered cautiously out of the reeds and saw two canoes moving towards them. In the front canoe were three soldiers and in the rear one sat Captain Tsen and an N.C.O. Hagen bared his teeth in a savage grin. He gently released Rose and said: 'Try and hang on for a few minutes more, angel. I promise you I'll get you out of this.'

'Jesus Christ, five of them,' Mason whispered.

Hagen patted the sub-machine-gun. 'Sitting ducks,' he said. 'I'll wait until I can't miss.'

The only sound was their own heavy breathing and the occasional bursts of conversation from the Chinese. Gradually the canoes drew near and Mason and Hagen moved forward to the very edge of the reeds. Hagen had never felt so calm, never felt so sure of anything in his life before. He couldn't miss. He raised the machine-gun and pulled the stock hard into his shoulder. His left eye closed and he squinted along the barrel. Almost before he realized it the first canoe was crossing his path. His finger tightened and a stream of bullets poured into the three soldiers and then as he swung towards the second canoe the gun went dead.

For one terrible moment he paused, reflected bitterly that you could never count on your luck to hold for very long, and then he hurled the useless weapon into the face of the N.C.O. who was sitting in front of Tsen. The man screamed and fell back, and

Tsen drew his pistol and fired wildly at Hagen. Mason threw himself out of the reeds and wrenched savagely at the side of the canoe, and as it turned over Captain Tsen took careful aim and shot him twice at close quarters.

The screaming N.C.O. had disappeared beneath the water. Hagen thrashed forward, groping for Mason's body, and Tsen surfaced beside him, terror in his eyes. Hagen grabbed him with his left hand and hammered the pock-marked face with his right fist. He gripped the Chinaman's throat firmly with both hands and forced his head back beneath the surface of the water. For a little while the body bucked agonizingly and then suddenly it was still. He released it and turned quickly towards Mason.

Rose was holding him with difficulty. Hagen grabbed at a floating paddle and pulled the nearest canoe forward. 'Hold the canoe steady,' he told her, 'I'll lift him in.'

Mason's eyes flickered and for a moment the familiar sardonic quirk touched his mouth. 'Don't waste your time,' he gasped, 'I've bought it this time.' Hagen lifted his head above the surface of the water. It seemed that Mason was trying to say something else and then a stream of blood issued from his mouth and his head jerked to one side.

For a brief moment Hagen still held him upright and then, as he heard the unmistakable sound of the launch returning, he released his grip and allowed Mason's body to sink beneath the surface. Rose screamed and surged forward, hammering at his face with her clenched fists. 'You can't leave him!' she screamed. 'Nothing matters to you! Nothing!'

For a moment he struggled with her and then in desperation, as the sound of the launch became louder, he slapped her heavily across the face several times. She hung limply in his grip, staring at him, the marks of his blows already beginning to show on her delicate skin. Suddenly her head dropped and she began to cry soundlessly, her shoulders heaving. He had no time for pity. He lifted her bodily and dumped her into the canoe, and then he scrambled carefully over the bow and groped for the paddle in the water, half-turning the canoe and sending it into the reeds on the far side.

He was not a moment too soon. They were barely under cover when the wash from the launch spread through the reeds lifting the canoe on a small wave. Hagen heard a startled cry and then the engine was cut. There were several more cries and then he heard Kossoff's voice and it sounded angry. He decided they must have discovered some of the bodies. He dropped the paddle and, slipping over the side, began to push the canoe forward by hand.

For several minutes he progressed in this way and Rose sat quietly in the middle of the canoe, her head bowed. Her spirit seemed utterly broken. He didn't think of her much. His mind was obsessed with the one idea – to survive. The canoe left the reeds suddenly, entering into a broad waterway, and he scrambled back in and began to paddle with all his strength.

There was an appreciable darkening in the sky and the sun was almost below the horizon. Hagen urged the canoe on furiously. He knew that if they were caught by darkness their one chance of finding *Hurrier* was lost. He kept bearing well to the east, and after twenty minutes of twisting and turning through several waterways came out into a large lagoon that seemed familiar. For a moment he rested, breathing heavily, his whole body aching with effort, and then a wild hope made him begin to paddle with a renewed vigour that sent the canoe skimming towards the end of the lagoon. He rested and they drifted forward silently. There was only the sound of the crickets through the quiet evening. He raised his voice and called, 'O'Hara – ahoy!'

For a little while he listened and then he heard O'Hara's cracked voice: 'Over here, lad. Over here!'

A sensation of utter relief and weariness flooded through Hagen. He dug the paddle into the water and sent the canoe cutting into the reeds in the direction O'Hara's voice had come from. He pulled on the reeds with his hands, forcing the canoe forward, and then they were through and moving across the quiet water towards *Hurrier*.

O'Hara leaned down and reached out his arms and Hagen lifted Rose up to him. He climbed wearily over the rail and stood swaying a little. And the old man said in a shocked voice, 'What happened to Mason?'

Hagen shook his head. 'He won't be back,' he said, and then Rose cried out sharply, as though in pain, and fainted.

Hagen reached forward and caught her in his arms. For a moment he sagged as his weary limbs protested and then he picked her up and said: 'I want you to get that other sub-machine-gun and stand watch, O'Hara. Kossoff's here and looking for us. I'm going to have a sleep. Wake me at midnight.'

He took Rose into her cabin and laid her down on her bunk. Very carefully he undressed her until she was completely naked and then he gently dried her soft young body. He did all this in a detached mood and his mind seemed to be on another level so that there was no desire and no craving. He wrapped her in several blankets and laid her back on the bunk. She stirred once and moaned a little, and then her head slipped to one side and she slept deeply.

Hagen stood looking down at her and then he turned away and stumbled into the other cabin. His feet tripped over something and he fell heavily against the table. When he looked down he saw the gold, neatly stacked on the floor. For some time he stared down at it and his brain tried to focus properly but nothing would fit into place. His conscious memory was like a jig-saw puzzle with all the pieces pulled apart and jumbled up together so that nothing made any sense. The bunk seemed to rise to meet him and he pitched head-foremost into the sleep of utter exhaustion.

He came back to life with difficulty and lay staring into the darkness for several minutes. When he swung his legs over the edge of the bunk he winced in sudden agony as pain coursed through the strained muscles of his body. His head felt heavy and there was a deadness to everything. He sat on the edge of the bunk for a few moments and then everything came back to him. For the moment the whole thing looked hopeless and he pushed himself upright and leaned on the table remembering, and it was not pleasant.

He had difficulty in co-ordinating his thoughts and with a deliberate and conscious effort he pushed the memories of the day's events back into the recesses of his mind and concentrated on the present. O'Hara – that was it. O'Hara should have awakened him. He cautiously felt his way through the cabin and went on deck.

The night sky was dark and there was no moon, but the stars glittered coldly except to the east where they were obscured by heavy cloud. He walked to the rail and stood listening to the small sounds of the night, and the rich, pungent stench of the marsh filled his nostrils and he felt better. A light mist curled over the water, obscuring the surface, and hope flickered in his mind. His hands gripped the rail convulsively and he peered at the mist and wondered if it would thicken.

Behind him he was aware of heavy breathing and then a small, broken snore. He crouched down and discovered O'Hara asleep, his head against the wheelhouse, an empty bottle of rum on the deck beside him.

For a moment anger lifted in Hagen's throat and then he relaxed completely, drained of all emotion. Charlie had been right in the beginning. You couldn't rely on a rum-soaked old man, not even when danger threatened. He left him there and moved to the wheelhouse to check the time. It was a little after one o'clock. He went back on deck and stood at the rail thinking, and he shivered suddenly as a small wind began to creak through the reeds with a sibilant whispering. He became aware for the first time that his clothing was still damp and he went back into the cabin and undressed quickly. He towelled his tender body briskly and pulled on dry pants and a heavy woollen sweater and moved quietly into the girl's cabin.

He listened for a moment to her regular breathing and then went into the galley and began to prepare coffee on the stove.

He covered the small port-holes with a blanket and turned on the light, and then he quietly brought all the remaining arms through from his cabin and began to check them. As he carefully reloaded the remaining sub-machine-gun there was a slight noise and he looked up sharply. Rose stood in the doorway. She was swathed in one of her blankets and somehow she looked completely defenceless. Her eyes had sunk back into their sockets and she looked desperately ill and exhausted. Hagen put down the weapon quickly and stood up. 'You look pretty rough,' he said. 'Sit here.' He gently moved her to a seat and went to the stove.

As he prepared the coffee she said: 'I want to apologize. I caused you a lot of trouble.' He ignored the opening and kept his back to her and she went on, 'I think I was almost out of my mind.' She coughed heavily and seemed to choke. 'I'll never forget the look on Steve's face when he disappeared under the water.'

Hagen turned and handed her a mug. 'I've put plenty of sugar in it,' he said. 'And I want you to take these pills.'

He took a small box from a drawer and handed her two capsules and she said suspiciously, 'What are they?'

'Don't worry,' he said, reassuringly, 'they're harmless. Benzedrine. They'll give you the energy necessary to get through the rest of this affair.'

She took the capsules without argument and washed them down with coffee. After a while she said, 'Mark, you're sure Steve was . . .'

Hagen nodded. 'He was dead before I let go of him. Tsen shot him twice at point-blank range. It was bad luck. Just one of those things.'

She laughed bitterly. 'Just one of those things? He was alive yesterday and now he's dead. That's all I know.'

Hagen lit a cigarette and took a brandy bottle from the cupboard. He poured a generous measure into his coffee and said slowly, 'Look, this may not help you, but Mason didn't think he stood a very good chance of getting back alive.'

She stared at him with tragic eyes and moaned: 'Then why? Why did he come?'

Hagen shrugged. 'He came for the same reason I did. Because it was his last chance. Because there wasn't anything else he could do.'

The silence was heavy and oppressive and she nervously squeezed her hands around the mug and said: 'Did he know – about the gold? That you were only going to give me a share and keep the rest?'

For a single moment Hagen was about to say no. To tell her that Mason at least had been honest with her, but the moment passed. Somewhere near at hand Mason seemed to smile sardonically and Hagen said: 'Everybody was in on it. They all wanted a share.'

She smiled harshly and stared blindly into space. 'What a fool I was. What a fool I was to believe you.'

He felt the thrust of that barbed charge as though it had penetrated his flesh. She held no one responsible but him. For her, the others were of no account. For a moment an un-reasoning anger moved in him and he turned and poured coffee into his cup with an unsteady hand. 'Did you really imagine that

259

men would risk suicide for wages when they could have so much more?'

'No – I was never so simple.' She stood up and placed the mug on the seat beside her. 'From the beginning it was an unbelievable dream. You were the reality. I believed in *you* – no other. I thought you were doing it because you loved me.' She walked quietly back into her cabin and closed the door.

For a little while he sat staring into space and thinking, and then he sighed and said, half aloud, 'What a damned pity it had to come too late.'

He finished loading the sub-machine-gun and the carbine and then he primed the remaining grenades. He counted them in satisfaction. There were eight and he smiled slightly. Kossoff was not going to take them so easily. As he stood up the door opened and the girl returned. She was wearing a spare pair of his pants with the bottoms rolled up and an old sweater. There was a subtle change in her appearance and it was nothing to do with clothes. She said briskly, 'What happens now?'

Hagen tucked the box of grenades under

one arm and picked up the weapons. 'I think you'd better make a meal,' he said. 'I'll take these to the wheelhouse.'

'Where's O'Hara?'

He smiled tightly. 'Drunk. I left him on watch and he's sprawled out on deck.'

She turned to the stove and said: 'You'd better bring him down here. I'll make more coffee and try to sober him up.'

When he had stowed the weapons safely in the wheelhouse he returned to O'Hara. He crouched down and shook him and, as the old man groaned, slapped him several times in the face. O'Hara came awake and struggled for a moment and Hagen held him firmly and said: 'Shut up, you old bastard. I don't want to hear a peep out of you.'

He jerked O'Hara to his feet and half-dragged him through into the galley and deposited him on a seat. The old man blinked and ran a blue-veined hand over his face. 'I don't feel very well,' he said.

'You'll feel a damned sight worse if you don't sober up,' Hagen told him.

Rose handed the old man a mug of strong, black coffee. 'Drink it. You'll feel better.'

He took the mug with trembling hands and spilled half of it down his shirt. Hagen snorted with disgust and said, 'I can't trust you for five minutes at a time.' Rose laughed lightly and when he looked at her she was smiling in a peculiar fashion. He turned quickly and went up on deck.

He went into the wheelhouse and turned on the tiny light above the chart table and began to make calculations. It was two-fifteen and the rendezvous with Charlie's boat was for six o'clock. He examined the chart again and then went out on deck and gazed at the water. The mist had thickened appreciably and swirled up from the marsh in ghostly waves. He flicked his cigarette into the night and a smile creased his face. He looked up at the sky and could see only half the stars that had been visible an hour before. When he went down into the galley there was hope on his face.

'You look pleased with yourself,' Rose said as she put a plate of beans in front of him.

He nodded. 'Things are looking up,' he said. 'There's a heavy mist beginning to rise.'

'Won't that make it more difficult for us?' she said. 'How will we ever get out of the marshes if we can't see where we're going?'

He helped himself to coffee and smiled. 'The quickest way out of this place is by the deep-water channels. I can follow those pretty well by chart.'

'It's going to be dangerous, lad,' O'Hara said. 'Those divils are bound to be waiting at the mouth of the Kwai.'

Hagen nodded. 'Sure they will, but we haven't got any choice. Our rendezvous is in three and a half hours. The only way we'll make it is by leaving this place the easy way.'

Rose sat down opposite him, a mug of coffee in her hands. 'Do you really think we can get away with it?' she said. Her voice was grave and steady and there was no hope in it.

He looked up and smiled. 'I think there's a chance. We'll have to play hide-and-seek in the mist, but remember – we've only got Kossoff to deal with, not the Chinese Navy. We know that now.'

She smiled and there was a surprising note of sadness in her voice as she said: 'You never give in, do you? What a man you could have been.'

For a moment their eyes locked and Hagen said sadly, 'We aren't always responsible for the way things work out.' She dropped her eyes and he lit a cigarette and said, 'I'm only asking for one more miracle and then I think we really do stand a chance.'

Suddenly there was a tapping on the roof overhead and Rose looked up in alarm, and then the tapping increased until a thousand fingers danced on the roof. Hagen got to his feet and ran quickly through the cabin and went on deck. He stood with his face upturned into the heavy rain and the girl stood beside him. He turned and laughed wildly down into her face. 'Well, there you are,' he said, 'the other miracle. Now I know we're going to get away with it.'

12

Hagen spent another half-hour with his charts, carefully calculating the route from the lagoon to the main channel of the Kwai. He decided to begin the journey at three forty-five. That would get them to the mouth of the Kwai in good time for the rendezvous, and the necessary speed would be so slow that the engines would hardly be audible in the heavy rain. O'Hara came to him in the wheelhouse, sober and contrite. He was full of apologies and Hagen cut him off short. 'All right. So you didn't mean any harm. Well for Christ's sake remember that we're facing the trickiest part of the whole deal during the next three hours. If you make a slip I swear

I'll drop you over the side and you can swim back.'

'You can trust me, lad,' O'Hara said, drawing himself up straight. 'I've never let you down at the crucial moment yet.'

Hagen laughed cynically. 'Not bloody much. Get down to the engine-room and make sure everything's perfect. You've got half an hour.'

He carefully re-checked his calculations and grunted with satisfaction. There was a chance. A damned good chance. He went below to the galley and found Rose clearing the place up. 'Is that necessary?' he said.

She wiped a plate and shrugged. 'It gives me something to do.'

He pushed a cigarette between his lips. 'I think we stand a chance. I really do.'

She showed no enthusiasm. 'I see.'

He smoked silently for a moment, watching her as she worked, and finally said, 'You don't seem very pleased.'

'Should I be? After all, what will success mean to me?'

'Oh, for God's sake,' Hagen said. 'Nobody

266

is trying to cheat you out of everything. If you have your own way you'll give everything to some crack-pot relief organization. If you play it my way you'll get a nice slice for yourself.' There was pity on her face and he turned away and said angrily, 'After all we've been through we deserve every damned penny of it.'

For a moment there was silence and then she moved behind him and put a hand on his arm. 'Can't you understand, Mark? It was a trust. My father died for it. I can't let him down.'

He shook his head in bewilderment. 'But you can't play the game that way, angel. Life isn't like that.'

She smiled sadly into his face. 'Then I'd rather not play at all.' She turned away and leaned on the table. When she spoke her voice was strong and hard, admitting no weakness. 'I'd rather see the gold back at the bottom of the sea than have it used for the wrong purpose.'

For a moment an angry retort was on his lips and then he cracked suddenly, and his shoulders sagged a little. There was a force here that he could not contend with on equal terms. He shook his head, an ironical smile on his lips, and said: 'Integrity and honour. I thought they'd gone out of fashion.' He grinned. 'Mason must be laughing his damned head off at me.'

She swung round and there was hope on her face. 'You'll help me, Mark? You'll help me to get the gold to Saigon?'

His face hardened and he shook his head slowly. 'Not a chance, angel. I can't afford your kind of ethics.'

Her shoulders sagged and she seemed to age ten years. 'I see.' She turned away and began to wipe another plate in a mechanical, defeated fashion.

Hagen said, 'Are you going to help us get out of here?'

She carefully put the last plate in the cupboard and turned towards him and he saw that there was a change in her. She was straight again and in full control. 'Yes, I'll help you.' She laughed bitterly. 'I'm trapped by my kind of ethics, you see. I'm thinking of that old man in the engine-room. If I refused to help you and we were caught, he would die, too, and I wouldn't like to have that on my conscience.'

For a moment they challenged each other and then Hagen turned away. 'If you'll come on deck, I'll show you what to do,' he said.

He gave her a heavy reefer coat as a protection against the rain, and a powerful electric torch. He took her forward to the prow and shone the torch out into the gloom. The heavy white beam lanced through the rain and mist and showed the reeds quite clearly on the far side of the lagoon. 'What do I have to do?' she said.

He explained. 'Stay here in the prow. We'll be going dead slow and I'll keep warning you when to look out for side channels. The waterways are pretty narrow and the torch should give you enough light. I don't want to use the spot.'

She nodded. 'Is that all?'

His smile was obscured by the night as he said: 'Don't bother about port and starboard. Just yell out right or left and then I'll know what you mean.' He turned on his heel and a thought struck him and he added: 'Hang on to the stay and be careful. I don't want you going over the side.'

Her voice came sadly from the darkness. 'Good luck, Mark.' For a brief moment he almost reached out his arms to her and then he turned quickly and went aft to the wheel-house.

It was nearly four o'clock when the engines shuddered into life and he took *Hurrier* forward and into the barrier of reeds. Slowly and relentlessly they passed through and out into the larger lagoon beyond. He turned the wheel sharply and the boat swirled obediently round and proceeded into the mist towards the sea.

Hagen opened the window of the wheel-house and rain kicked into his face. There was a slight wind blowing in from the sea, across the marshes, lifting the mist before it into weird shapes, and he could taste the salt of it on his lips. Very slowly and carefully the boat ploughed forward into the darkness, her engines no more than a dull rumble as though they slept. Hagen consulted his chart. At their present speed they should be approaching the first cut-off. He leaned out of the window and hailed the girl. 'Any minute now on your left there should be a channel.'

For a few minutes there was nothing, only the beam of her torch stabbing into the darkness ahead, and then she cried out and Hagen began to swing the wheel. The prow of the launch grazed a wall of reeds and he swung the wheel even further and then quickly spun it in his hands to straighten her, and they were proceeding safely along the new course.

They repeated the manœuvre on three occasions without serious mishap. Only once did they overshoot and Hagen was compelled to reverse, but the time lost was of no consequence. Gradually a faint, pearly luminosity appeared and he was able to distinguish the greyness of the mist and then the dark, silver lances of the rain. On the next occasion he had to change course he was able to distinguish the turning for himself. He leaned out of the window and shouted to the girl: 'You can finish now. I can see well enough myself.'

She came aft and stood looking up at him. 'I'm soaked,' she said. 'I'm going below to change.'

Through the driving rain and the mist visibility was down to twenty yards, but the reeds were beginning to drop back and the channel was widening perceptibly. The water began to lift in long, swelling ripples, and waves kicked against the bottom of the launch. The wind was increasing and he turned into it, and knew that they were in the main channel of the Kwai and that a mile before them lay the open sea.

He slowed the engines even more until *Hurrier* crept forward in almost complete silence and the roaring of the rain was the loudest thing that was to be heard. He lit a cigarette and closed the window and held the wheel lightly between his hands. It was almost over. He felt supremely confident. It was as if the whole thing had been planned from the very beginning. Even the mist and the rain had appeared right on time.

The whole thing was perfect and still he felt lousy. He found himself wishing the girl had been different. If only she'd been tougher, more worldly, it wouldn't have been so bad. As it was he felt as though he had taken advantage of a child. He wondered what would become of her after all this was over. He was going to have to force her share of the gold on her, but he was prepared for that. He knew that the real trouble lay in the fact that she might refuse to use it. Might even give it away. If she did that then her final end was plain and she didn't have the sort of toughness needed to survive. There was only one end for penniless girls in Macao, and suddenly he cursed and slammed his clenched fist against the wall. He couldn't see her turned loose on her own. She wasn't fit to look after herself. The door opened and she entered, carrying a mug of coffee. He smiled and took it gratefully. 'Thanks! I needed this.'

'How are we doing?'

'Not so bad. We're in the main channel out of the marshes. The tricky part comes later.' He locked the wheel and pulled the chart over and showed her. 'The mouth of the channel is pretty well ringed by sandbanks. The final outlet to the sea is rather narrow. If Kossoff is ahead of us, and I'm hoping he isn't, he'll be waiting there.'

She nodded and said seriously, 'Won't it be dangerous trying to get through the narrows?'

He shrugged. 'It depends. If he is there, then I'll have to think of something else.' He studied the chart and added: 'Once we reach the open sea our worries are over. *Hurrier* will show a clean pair of heels to that tub of Kossoff's, unless he's got something pretty special in the engine-room.'

'And afterwards?' she said.

He shrugged. 'Plain sailing. Charlie's freighter should be on time. The weather's been calm enough.'

'What about *Hurrier*?' Rose said. 'What will happen to her?'

His face tightened. 'I'm afraid she'll have to go down.'

'Mark!' There was shocked surprise in her voice. 'You wouldn't sink her?'

'Why not?' he said. 'I can't do anything

else. I'm damned if I'm going to leave her for Kossoff and his pals. I'd rather see her at the bottom of the sea – and believe me, it's deep enough off this coast. When she goes down she'll go a long way.'

She leaned against the window and stared out into the rain. 'It's rather sad, isn't it?' she said. 'A boat must seem like a real person when you've had her for a long time.'

Hagen smiled sombrely. 'If I could save her I would but I can't risk that return trip. Not with the gold on board, anyway.' He laughed suddenly. 'It could be worse. After all, I shan't need her after this morning. I'll be living in a different world.'

She said quietly: 'What will you do? Where will you go – America?'

He shook his head. 'No, I don't think so. Too many people I know.' He chuckled. 'I wouldn't be welcomed in polite society.' He lit another cigarette and said: 'I think Europe would be the place. Not England – killed by taxes these days. Switzerland or Ireland.' His voice warmed. 'Probably Ireland. Now there's a grand country for you.'

'What will you be – a country squire?' There was a hint of laughter in her voice.

He grinned. 'That's about it, I think. A quiet country place near the sea will suit me, and the world can go on without me. I've had enough of the worst of it to last me for the rest of my life.'

She nodded slowly and said: 'Yes, I don't blame you. It's a nice dream.'

A wave of tenderness ran through him. He turned and looked at her and the sadness that showed in her face went to his heart. 'Come with me, angel,' he said urgently. 'We can make it together. It doesn't have to stay a dream.'

She shook her head. 'No, Mark! No, it can't be.' She turned away from him and gripped the handle of the door convulsively.

'But why not?' he said. 'I can't leave you flat in Macao. You'd always be on my mind.'

'So you feel responsible for me?' she said. 'Why should you?'

'It isn't only that.' He felt suddenly awkward. 'There's more to it than that.'

He reached out a hand and touched her

shoulder and she pulled away sharply. 'No, it's no good, Mark. You see, I love you. I thought that was enough but it isn't. I now find that I need to respect you as well, and as things stand I can't.' She wrenched open the door before he could reply and was gone.

For a little while he leaned heavily on the wheel and stared with blind eyes into the rain and thought about her. It wasn't pretty but then he'd known in his heart from the beginning that he was playing her a dirty trick. He straightened up and shrugged the thoughts away. To hell with it. It was done and that was that. He'd offered her a share and she would get it whether she wanted it or not. After that she would have to look out for herself. He turned to check the time and the engines spluttered, coughed asthmatically, and died.

There was a sudden, terrible silence and for a moment Hagen stood gripping the wheel, the only sound the drumming of the rain on the roof of the wheelhouse, and then he cursed and went on deck.

As he passed the cabin door Rose poked

her head out, alarm on her face. 'What's up?' she demanded.

He waved a hand. 'How the hell would I know?' he said and dropped down the ladder into the engine-room.

O'Hara was on his knees in one corner and when Hagen knelt beside him he turned a glum face. 'One of the fuel pipes, lad,' he said.

Hagen had a look. 'Bloody hell, that's all we needed,' he said. The pipe had a crack several inches long in it.

'That's what comes of trusting wog traders,' O'Hara told him. 'I remember you getting that pipe from an Indian in Hong Kong and it was half the usual price.'

Hagen snorted. 'Who the hell cares about that now. For God's sake get moving. Try binding it with tape. It only has to hold for another half an hour or so.' He got to his feet and scrambled up the ladder on to the deck.

Rose wiped rain away from her face with the back of a hand and said, 'Is it bad?'

'Bad enough,' Hagen told her. 'My own

fault. I put a cheap pipe in a few months back when I was a bit short. The damned thing was faulty. It's cracked.'

'Can it be fixed?'

He nodded. 'O'Hara's having a go at it now. He might fix it enough to get us where we're going.'

She gazed over his shoulder and gave a cry of alarm. 'Quick, Mark. We're running aground.'

He whirled round and saw the long, low back of a sandbank stretching towards them from the mist. He ran to the wheelhouse and turned the wheel and the current pushed them gently towards the bank. There was a slight shudder and they came to a standstill. He went back on deck and reassured the girl. 'Don't worry,' he said. 'The engines will pull us off with no trouble. We're better off here than drifting.'

He turned towards the engine-room hatch and as he put a foot on the ladder Rose cried, 'Stop!' He turned in surprise and she said, 'I thought I heard something.'

They stood at the rail, listening together,

and gradually Hagen became aware, through the mist and rain, of the unmistakable sound of an engine that drew closer every second. Rose turned to speak and he motioned her to silence. Gradually the noise increased until it seemed to be almost on top of them and then it began to grow fainter. Through the mist a distinct ripple ran through the water and splashed against the hull. Hagen whistled. 'My God, that was close.' Before she could reply the engine of the other boat was suddenly cut and there was silence.

Rose said: 'What does it mean? Why have they stopped?'

He stood thinking for a moment and then he went back to the wheelhouse and looked at the chart. After a moment he began to take off his reefer jacket. 'I don't think we're all that near to the outlet,' he said.

Rose spoke over his shoulder. 'What are you going to do?' He pulled off his shoes and went past her out on to the deck. 'Mark, what are you doing?' There was fear in her voice.

The deck was cold to his feet and as the

rain spattered on his bare shoulders he shivered. 'I'm going for a little swim,' he said. 'Don't worry. I know what I'm doing.' He lowered himself over the rail down into the water. It was bitterly cold and then his feet touched the sand and he smiled up into her frightened face and turned away.

He waded out of the water on to the sandbank and followed its length into the mist until he could no longer see *Hurrier*. He began to trot and the blood moved in his body again. Twice he had to wade through deep water but the going was comparatively easy. After walking and wading for some six or seven minutes he heard voices. He stood quite still and listened carefully and after a while he continued, but more cautiously. He heard a voice again, this time far out in the mist to his left. He waded into the water and began to swim.

It was bitterly cold and a strong current tugged at his body. The current was stronger than he had thought and he was about to turn back when a shape loomed out of the mist ahead. It was Kossoff's launch. For a moment

Hagen floated, watching it, and then he turned and began to swim back.

It was hard work fighting the current and for a few ghastly moments he thought he had made an error and then his feet dragged in shallow water and the sandbank lifted before him. He began to run at a steady pace and it was several minutes before he came to his original footprints where he had entered the water. He paused for a moment and through the mist there came a shattering roar as the engines of Kossoff's launch broke into life. The sound of the launch slowly faded in the direction of the sea and Hagen began to run again, splashing through the water as the tide began to lift over the sandbank.

It took him longer than he had imagined to return to the launch, and for a little while he thought he had made a mistake. The mist seemed to have thickened a little, and it was with a sense of relief that he saw *Hurrier* materialize. He splashed through the deepening water and pulled himself over the rail. Rose and O'Hara were both waiting anxiously on deck. He brushed aside their questions and went straight into the wheel-house and examined the chart. He suddenly felt a blanket on his shoulders and turned and smiled his thanks to Rose. 'It was cold out there,' he said.

'Did you see the other boat?'

He nodded. 'Yes, it was Kossoff. Don't know why he stopped. He'll be waiting at the mouth of the Kwai for us.'

O'Hara groaned. 'Then it looks bad,' he said.

Hagen traced a finger across the chart and gave a grunt of satisfaction. 'There's a channel here. It's pretty shallow in places but the tide is in and that might make a difference.' He nodded and said in an abstracted way, 'I'll have to do some more wading though.'

'Why?' Rose demanded. 'It's dangerous and the water's icy. You'll get pneumonia.'

He shrugged. 'It's got to be done,' he told her. 'I'll have to go ahead and find the deepest part of the channel. You can't rely on this chart – the sands have a habit of shifting.'

'Will we miss Kossoff altogether if we can get through by this other channel?' she said.

He frowned and considered the point. 'If we're lucky we might. We'll come out very close to the main channel. So close that if it wasn't for the mist it wouldn't be worth it. He'd be bound to spot us. Let's hope it keeps up.'

O'Hara had listened with a worried expression on his face and now he spoke. 'I've managed to tape that pipe, lad, but it won't last for long. Wherever we're going we'd better get there soon.'

Hagen clapped him on the shoulder. 'We'll get there, O'Hara. Take the wheel and follow me through the shoals. Whatever happens keep her dead slow and watch me like a hawk. If we get stuck in this lot we'll be a sitting duck for Kossoff when the mist lifts.'

He threw off the blanket and smiled at Rose and then vaulted over the rail into the water. The channel he was seeking was a hundred yards back along the sandbank on which he was walking. O'Hara started the engines and reversed *Hurrier* off the sandbank and turned her round in a smooth curve that had her finally making a parallel course to Hagen. The sandbank dipped under the water and Hagen went cautiously forward until the water was at chest level. He waved his arms and beckoned and O'Hara brought the boat round in a tight curve and she slowly entered the channel.

Hagen swam forward into the shoals, sounding for bottom with his feet every few yards. Behind him *Hurrier* came steadily on, carefully following his circuitous trail. It was bitterly cold, and after twenty minutes he felt completely numb. Finally, even his brain was affected and he carried on sounding with his feet and followed the channel, using a kind of blind instinct born of desperation and necessity. Once the launch grounded on a sandbank when the channel took a particularly sudden twist, but O'Hara managed to refloat her with little difficulty.

Hagen became aware that the water was lifting into his face and suddenly he lost bottom and had to swim in earnest. His leaden limbs moved slowly and he dipped under the water and panic gripped him, and then something bumped against him and hands reached down and grabbed him by the hair. He blindly lifted an arm and his hand was seized, and then he was hauled up and over the rail and subsided on the deck.

O'Hara was grinning down at him, his lips drawn back, exposing his foul old teeth. 'You've done it, lad,' he cackled. 'You've done that bastard in the eye.'

'Christ, but I'm cold,' Hagen said and Rose wrapped a blanket around him. He scrambled to his feet and said to O'Hara: 'Full speed ahead. Give her everything she's got. Doesn't matter about the noise. Kossoff will never catch us in that tub of his.' The old man grinned and gave a mock salute and Hagen painfully went below.

There was coffee brewing on the stove, and as he pulled on dry pants and a sweater Rose poured some in a mug and added brandy. 'Here, drink this,' she said. 'I don't know how you managed to stand it.'

The whole boat shuddered and lifted suddenly as O'Hara took her forward quickly at full power. The noise of the engines deepened into a steady roar and Hagen grinned and raised his mug. 'A sailor's farewell to Comrade Kossoff,' he said, and as he placed the mug to his lips the engines missed a couple of times, spluttered, tried to pick up and then died completely.

The girl's face turned deathly white in the silence which followed, and Hagen carefully put the mug down on the table and stood up. 'If the bastard doesn't get us now,' he said, 'he doesn't deserve to.' He passed quickly out of the galley and went up on deck.

13

Hagen dropped into the engine-room and found O'Hara on his knees in the corner. There was a stench of burning oil and the old man's face was grey with fear. Hagen crouched down beside him. 'What's happened?' he said.

O'Hara wiped sweat from his forehead with an oily rag. 'The crack's lengthened,' he said. 'Engine vibration. It was only to be expected.'

Hagen cursed softly and wiped the pipe clean so that he could examine it. He nodded slowly and sat back on his heels. 'Doesn't look so good.'

'What can we do, lad?' the old man said, and there was despair in his voice.

There was a sound of movement on deck and Rose looked in through the hatch. 'Will it be all right, Mark?' she said anxiously.

He shrugged and replied: 'Can't tell yet. Any sign of action up there?'

She shook her head. 'Not a thing. I can't even hear the launch.'

He came to a sudden decision. 'How long would it take to unscrew the pipe and braze it?'

O'Hara frowned and shook his head. 'Too long, lad. Ten minutes to get it out. About twenty to braze it and another ten to replace it.'

Hagen nodded. 'About forty minutes. That's not so bad. Get moving.'

'It's too long,' O'Hara's voice rose, high-pitched and frightened. 'We're like a sitting duck here.'

Hagen grabbed him by the shoulders and shook him viciously. 'Get some sense,' he said. 'If we tape the whole damned pipe it might last twenty minutes, but what if the freighter doesn't show up? Anything could happen.'

He released his grip and O'Hara nodded

dumbly for a moment and then said, 'You're right.' He breathed deeply and squared his shoulders. 'Don't worry, lad, I'll get it done. You'd better get on deck in case of trouble.'

Hagen smiled reassuringly and clapped him on the shoulder. 'Don't worry,' he said, 'we'll make it. We haven't come this far to throw in the sponge.'

He scrambled up on to the deck and as he appeared, Rose said: 'Listen, Mark. I think I hear something.'

The boat lifted on the swell and the only sound was the slapping of the waves against her bows. He stood at the rail, ears straining, and away in the distance he heard the sound of an engine. He gripped the rail with both hands and waited. 'Tell O'Hara to make as little noise as possible,' he said.

Rose disappeared down the engine-room hatch and Hagen went into the wheelhouse and got the sub-machine-gun. He stood at the rail and listened as the sound of the engine drew nearer and, after a while, it was very close and unmistakable. Rose stood at his side. 'Is it Kossoff?' she said.

Hagen nodded and said bitterly: 'Sounds like his launch. He must have heard us.'

She nodded. 'I don't suppose he could have missed hearing.' There was a quality of finality in her tone. 'What will he do?' she said.

He crooked the sub-machine-gun in one arm and lit a cigarette, his hands cupped against the wind. 'It's pretty obvious. He'll know that one of two things has happened. Either we've broken down or we're meeting somebody. He has a rough idea where we are. Now all he has to do is sweep backwards and forwards through the mist until he finds us.'

She turned her troubled face and gazed out anxiously into the mist and they listened as the sound of the launch drew nearer and nearer. Once it passed very close indeed. For a moment Hagen had a wild hope that Kossoff had missed them, that there was still a chance and then, suddenly, the noise of the engine lifted and the launch charged out of the mist. He pushed Rose roughly on to the deck and crouched beside the rail.

The launch came straight towards them and then veered slightly at the last moment and cut across their stern. Suddenly the air was violent with the chatter of a machine-gun and Hagen ducked low as bullets swept across the deck. The wheelhouse rocked and glass splintered, and then he jumped to his feet and fired a long burst at the two men who crouched at the machine-gun in the rear of Kossoff's launch. There was a strangled scream, and as the launch disappeared into the mist he had the satisfaction of seeing one of them lurch to the rail and topple into the sea.

The sound of the launch faded and he shouted to Rose: 'Get below. Next time he'll pour it on hot.' He ran to the wheelhouse and pulled out the box containing the grenades.

The launch seemed to make a broad sweep and circled in the mist several times. Hagen waited impatiently and was aware of Rose crouching beside him with the carbine in her hands. Before he could argue with her, the launch moved rapidly out of the mist and came towards them again. There were another two men behind the gun and this time Hagen started the shooting. He raked their wheelhouse in the blind hope that Kossoff might be in there, and then he threw himself flat on the deck as another hail of lead swept across the rail. Again the launch veered sharply, and as it cut across their bows, Hagen lobbed a grenade neatly over the rail on to the deck. As the launch swerved, heeling over, the grenade rolled towards the rail, but before it bounced into the water it exploded. A wave swept over the stern of the launch, and when it cleared, the machine-gun and the two soldiers had disappeared. The launch ran on into the mist and suddenly there was quiet.

Rose wiped blood from her face and said, 'I think a splinter caught me.'

He turned quickly, concern leaping inside him. 'Here, let me have a look.' There was a deep cut in one cheek. 'Come into the wheelhouse. I'll put a plaster on it.'

O'Hara poked his head out of the hatch. 'Are we still in one piece?' he demanded.

'Get back on the job,' Hagen snarled.

The old man disappeared back into the engine-room and Hagen took the girl into the wheelhouse. He pulled out a splintered drawer and found a tin of surgical tape. 'This will have to do for now,' he said. He cut off a strip and placed it over the deep cut. 'There, how's that?'

She smiled wanly. 'Better, but what's going to happen now?'

He lit a cigarette and blew out the smoke steadily. 'I don't think he'll come dashing in again like that in a hurry,' he said. 'For one thing, that grenade must have shaken him, and anyway – he can't risk sinking us. That would mean no gold.' He walked out on deck and stared into the mist. 'No, we'll just have to wait for his next move and hope that O'Hara can mend that pipe.'

Visibility was still down to about thirty yards and the rain, which had slackened a little, suddenly increased. It was with a momentary sense of astonishment that he suddenly heard his name being called loudly from the mist. 'Captain Hagen! Why don't you give in? You can't get away.'

He reassured Rose. 'He's using a loud hailer.' He grinned tightly. 'I wonder what the bastard's playing at?' He raised his voice and called, 'Nothing doing, Kossoff!'

For a few moments there was silence and Hagen wondered whether his reply had been heard and then the Russian spoke again. 'Really, my friend, you are acting rather foolishly. Surely you don't wish the young lady to come to harm?'

Hagen said softly to Rose: 'There's something fishy going on. It sounds as if he's stalling for time. I wonder if he's got something up his sleeve.'

Again Kossoff's voice sounded. 'Come now, Captain.' There was a touch of impatience in his tone. 'Let us act sensibly. All I ask is the gold. You may have your lives.'

There was a slight bump against the hull of *Hurrier*, and Rose whirled round and screamed, 'Mark, look out behind you!'

Hagen pivoted and fired from the hip. The man who was already on deck was lifted back over the rail. The gun suddenly ceased firing and he dropped it with a curse and closed with the second soldier who half-fell as he scrambled over the rail. The man subsided with a groan and Hagen lifted his inanimate body and threw it into the sea. A small dinghy bobbed in the water and he quickly secured it with a length of rope to the rail.

The girl was white and frightened. Her voice trembled when she said, 'I can't take much more of this.'

Before Hagen could reply the engine of Kossoff's launch suddenly roared through the mist. As he turned, crouching, the launch cut across their prow and raked the deck with small-arms fire. He had only time to sweep Rose down beside the engine-room hatch and protect her with his body. The sound of the launch faded into the distance and he scrambled to his feet and lifted up the girl. 'Are you all right?'

'Yes, a bit shaken, but I'll manage.'

He moved quickly into the shattered wheel-house to reload the sub-machine-gun and stopped short in the doorway and looked at the interior. The walls were riddled with bullet holes and the wheel was badly splintered.

The instrument panel was shattered and for a moment fear gripped him, so that he could not move, and then he stepped forward and examined the controls. Rose said anxiously from the doorway, 'Is everything all right?'

He sighed with relief. 'The steering mechanism still works and that's the main thing.'

He moved out on to the deck again and slipped a fresh magazine into the gun. Rose said, 'We can't go on like this for much longer.'

There was a touch of fear in her tone and her voice trembled slightly. He turned to speak to her and then Kossoff's voice came through the rain again. 'Now then, Captain, have you come to your senses yet?' Hagen made no reply and the voice continued: 'It's obvious that you're incapable of moving, but I'll be generous. I'll give you fifteen minutes to think it over. Fifteen minutes, my friend. Think fast.' His voice died away and there was only the rain, hissing down into the water.

Hagen turned to the hatch and called down to O'Hara, 'How long now?'

The old man straightened up, a flaring

torch in one hand, and wiped sweat from his face. 'I'm still brazing,' he said. 'Almost finished. Fifteen or twenty minutes. I can't be sure.'

Hagen turned slowly to the rail. It was too bad but a man's luck always ran out sooner or later. He should have remembered that. He stood staring out into the mist in the direction of Kossoff's launch, defeated and despairing, and then he remembered. He slammed his hand against the rail. 'We've got one chance,' he said and there was hope in his voice. 'It's a slim one but it might work.' He turned to Rose. 'Ask O'Hara for that spare coil of wire cable – it's in the engine-room somewhere – and be quick.'

He ran down into the cabin and when he reappeared he was carrying the box that contained his diving gear. As he opened the box Rose arrived with the cable. 'Is this what you want?' she said. Hagen nodded and pulled off his sweater. 'What are you going to do?' she said. 'You can't risk swimming out there.'

He slipped his arms through the straps of the aqua-lung. 'I haven't any choice,' he said.

For a moment he thought she would argue and then she smiled tightly and said: 'All right, Mark. Have it your own way.' She started to tighten his straps.

When he was ready Hagen stood up. 'Now listen carefully because there isn't any time for repeats. I'll tie the end of the cable around one wrist and you pay it out as I go. I've got a little of that plastic explosive left and I'm going to try and fix Kossoff once and for all.'

'God help you,' she said as he quickly fastened detonators to the cable and tied it round his right wrist and then buckled the belt of explosives about his waist.

He went over the side quickly. For a brief second he looked up at her and she shivered and forced a smile to her face, and then he adjusted his valves and sank beneath the surface.

He had only the rough direction of the launch to go on but he knew that it was not far away. Probably just out of range of visibility. He swam very fast, kicking strongly with his rubber flippers, and it only took him two or three minutes to penetrate the mist. He sounded slowly and looked about him. There was no sign of the launch, and then suddenly his luck changed again and Kossoff's voice boomed out of the mist very close at hand. 'You have only eight minutes, Captain. Eight minutes.'

Hagen quickly submerged again and changed direction slightly and then the keel of the launch loomed through the water, and a moment later he was working his way along to the stern. He quickly fixed the adhesive plastic to a spot on the hull just below the propellor. He tied the cable round the rudder itself and forced the detonators into the explosive. The whole operation had taken him only two or three minutes. He turned quickly and began to follow the line of cable back towards *Hurrier*.

In his excitement and fear he didn't notice the cold, and from some inner reserve he drew forth additional power that sent him forging through the water faster than he had ever done. The cable lifted and he was bumping against the hull of the boat and Rose reached down a hand and Hagen cried: 'No! Detonate it now.'

As he pulled himself over the rail she feverishly clipped the cable and inserted the ends in the detonating box. From somewhere in the mist Kossoff's voice said, 'I'm sorry, my friend, but my patience has run out.'

There was the sudden coughing of the launch's engines as they warmed into life and then Rose depressed the plunger. The explosion echoed through the rain, and mingled with it were the screams of the dying. For a long time debris continued to spatter down into the water and then there was silence. O'Hara emerged from the engine-room hatch and said in a shaky voice: 'Holy Mother of God. She must have gone down like a stone.'

Hagen slowly unfastened the straps of the aqua-lung. 'It must have blown the stern clean out,' he said. He pulled off his flippers and stood up. 'How are things below?'

O'Hara managed a tired grin. 'Not that it matters now, but I've finished it.'

Hagen nodded slowly. He felt inexpressibly weary and more than a little light-headed.

He went below and dried himself and pulled on a sweater and then Rose called, 'Mark, come quickly!'

As he moved out on to the deck he heard his name being called faintly from the water. He went to the rail and at that moment Kossoff came swimming out of the mist. They all stood and watched the Russian approach and finally he floated in the water, bumping against the hull. His face looked yellow and old and he was half frozen. He managed a smile, and said, 'I always underestimated you, my friend.'

Hagen shook his head. 'I was lucky and you weren't,' he said. 'It was as simple as that.'

Kossoff gulped and swallowed a mouthful of water. When he finally managed to speak he said, 'You wouldn't leave me to drown?'

For a moment Hagen wanted to tell him to sheer off and then Rose touched his arm. 'Mark, we can't leave him.' He shrugged and reached a hand down to Kossoff and pulled him aboard.

The Russian sprawled on deck, coughing

and gasping for breath. 'Thank you,' he managed to say. 'You'll never regret it.'

Hagen laughed shortly. 'I wonder,' he said and turned to move towards the wheelhouse.

Behind him there was a sudden flurry of movement and Rose screamed, 'Look out!' and threw herself against him so that he went sprawling on to the deck.

He scrambled to his feet and turned quickly. She stood between him and the Russian and suddenly she swayed and fell backwards. Hagen jumped forward and caught her in his arms and there was blood on her breast. Kossoff backed away, a knife in his right hand, and said calmly, 'Even at the end I seem to be fated to have bad luck with you, Captain.'

Before Hagen could make a move O'Hara appeared from the wheelhouse with the sub-machine-gun in his hands. 'You murdering bastard,' he cried. 'She was worth ten of you.' He pressed the trigger and a stream of bullets hammered Kossoff over the rail and into the water. When O'Hara relaxed his finger the gun was empty.

Hagen lifted her gently in his arms and carried her down into the cabin. He laid her on her bunk and slipped a pillow under her head. As he moved to leave she gripped his arm fiercely. 'No, don't go. Don't leave me.'

He released himself as gently as he could and reassured her. 'I'm only going for the first-aid box.' She subsided against the pillow and he went into the galley.

When he returned O'Hara was bending over her. 'She's passed out,' the old man said.

Hagen brushed him aside and sat on the edge of the bunk. With a pair of surgical scissors he carefully cut open her sweater and the shirt she wore beneath it. Gently he pulled away the blood-stained material and O'Hara gasped suddenly as the wound was bared. Hagen swabbed away the blood with a wad of cotton wool and examined the wound. 'She's lucky,' he said. 'The point bounced off her collar-bone.' The slash ran diagonally from her left shoulder down into the breast.

'It looks bad,' O'Hara said. 'It looks damned bad.'

Hagen wiped sweat from his forehead with

the back of his hand. It was bad and the blood was pumping out of her at a frightening rate. He had to do something drastic before it was too late. 'Get on deck and start the engines,' he told O'Hara. 'I'll be up in a few minutes.'

The old man went without a word and Hagen packed the wound with pads of cotton wool and lint and bandaged it roughly, looping the bandage under her armpit and around her neck. She lay quietly and never stirred. For a moment he looked down at her and then he left the cabin.

The engines rumbled into life as he came on deck. The water was being whipped into white-caps by a strong east wind that blew steadily out to sea, carrying the mist before it, and visibility was becoming better minute by minute. He went into the wheelhouse and took over from O'Hara. 'We've got to move fast,' he said, 'or she'll bleed to death.'

'What do you intend to do?' O'Hara asked.

Hagen opened the throttle and took *Hurrier* forward in a surge of speed. 'There's that rocky island about a quarter of a mile from here,' he said. 'It has a good inlet. We'll anchor and I'll do a proper job on the shoulder.'

He took everything that the engines had to give him and the boat lifted out of the water like some great sea-bird. 'Starboard, lad, starboard!' O'Hara cried suddenly and Hagen spun the wheel and turned towards the island that was dimly visible through the mist and rain.

He cut the engines and let the boat run gently into the tiny inlet and O'Hara, waiting his chance, jumped on to the rocks as the boat bumped against them, and looped a line around a large boulder. Hagen braced himself and went below.

He put a kettle of water on the stove and then went quietly into the cabin and examined Rose. Blood was seeping through the bandages and he cursed softly and went back into the galley and lit a cigarette with hands that trembled slightly. He stood impatiently waiting for the kettle to boil and, when it was finally ready, poured the water into a basin which he carried into the cabin. He washed his hands carefully and bathed them in disinfectant, and O'Hara stood at the end of the bunk and said, 'What are you going to do?'

'Stitch it,' Hagen said briefly.

He sat down on the edge of the bunk and started to cut away the bandages and Rose slowly opened her eyes and smiled at him. 'Will I be all right, Mark?' she asked him.

He nodded. 'You're going to be fine, angel. Just leave everything to me.'

She closed her eyes again and O'Hara said, diffidently, 'Is there anything I can do?'

Hagen nodded. 'Wash your hands and then stand by my side. I want you to swab away the blood while I'm working.'

He carefully pulled away the last remnants of the bandages and wiped the wound clean and then he took out the glass ampoule that contained the needle and gut and broke it open. As blood welled brightly from the wound he said to O'Hara, 'Start swabbing.'

Rose opened her eyes. 'I love you, Mark,' she said.

Hagen smiled. 'I know and I'm going to hurt you.'

She shook her head. 'It doesn't matter. You've hurt me before.'

He nodded soberly. 'This will be the last time, I promise you.'

He leaned forward and examined the wound. For a moment he hesitated. She smiled weakly and said, 'Get on with it, darling,' and then she closed her eyes.

He wiped the sweat from his face and started. Mercifully, she fainted at the first touch of the needle. It took fifteen stitches to close that gaping wound, and when he had finished he was mentally and physically exhausted. He carefully looped round the last circle of bandage and fastened the ends in position with surgical tape. 'Well, that's it,' he sighed in relief.

'Will she be all right?' O'Hara demanded in a weak voice.

Hagen stood up. 'She's lost a lot of blood but she's young. She'll be fine.'

He took his binoculars and went up on deck. He jumped from the prow on to the boulder and scrambled up the rocks until he had reached a suitable vantage point and then he scanned the sea and the coastline through the binoculars. The mist had disappeared completely, blown to shreds by the strong wind. He could see Charlie's freighter coming from a long way off. It steamed slowly towards the position where Kossoff's launch had gone down, and through the binoculars Hagen could see the sailors lining the rail, peering down at the wreckage in the water as they passed. The freighter didn't decrease speed. It kept right on going in the direction of Macao and he watched it until it was almost out of sight. After a while there was a discreet cough and he turned to find O'Hara beside him. 'That was Charlie's boat?' the old man said.

Hagen nodded. 'That's right.' He scrambled down the rocks and O'Hara followed.

'Would I be right in supposing we're not returning to Macao at all?'

For a moment Hagen hesitated, but only for a moment. 'That's about the size of it,' he said. 'Do you mind?'

A grin split O'Hara's face wide open. 'She's a grand lass,' he said.

'Let's hope they thought that wreckage was all that was left of us,' Hagen said.

O'Hara nodded, suddenly sober. 'I hope so. Charlie has a long arm.'

Hagen went into the wheelhouse and started the engines. He reversed out of the inlet and then turned the wheel over to O'Hara. 'I think we can just about make Haiphong,' he said. 'You take over for a while. I'll relieve you later.'

He went below and sat by her bunk, smoking and looking at her, and after a while she opened her eyes and smiled at him. The cabin tilted as *Hurrier* lunged into the waves and she said weakly, 'We're moving again?' He nodded and she went on, 'Macao?'

He shook his head. 'Haiphong. We've got just enough fuel. We'll move on to Saigon from there.'

For a moment she lay watching him and the tears began to well slowly from her eyes. 'Oh, Mark, I love you so much.'

He leaned over and kissed her gently on the cheek. 'When I was patching you up,' he said, 'a funny thing happened. I forgot about the gold. In fact, I forgot about everything except you.'

'What about Charlie?' she said.

'To hell with Charlie. We'll turn over the gold and sell the boat and move on. I'm not afraid of Charlie.'

'Where will we go?' she said. 'Ireland?'

He nodded. 'Maybe; we'll talk about it.'

She smiled happily and he took her hand, and after a time she drifted into sleep. He sat there for a little while longer, and then he went up on deck and took over the wheel from O'Hara.

The wind had freshened even more and spray spattered against the shattered windows of the wheelhouse as the boat dipped over the waves. A gull flew low over the deck and skimmed the water with a shrill cry, and as the wheel kicked in his hand Hagen suddenly grinned. For the first time in his life he felt as if he was really breaking out of something.